W9-BFH-953

The Ghostly Eyeball

Tim started to climb the winding steps.

But before he could get very far, there was a sudden rumbling sound from deep in the earth. The floor shook. A crack opened in the rock, and something emerged that made Tim want to run home and hide under his bed.

It was an eyeball.

A flying eyeball!

Unlike other eyeballs, however, this one was gigantic, with a huge mouth filled with nasty sharp teeth — as well as two arms covered with claws!

"I see you!" said the eyeball.

Other Worlds of Power books
you will enjoy:

Blaster Master®
Metal Gear®
Ninja Gaiden®
Wizards & Warriors®

CASTLEVANIA II
SIMON'S QUEST®

A novel based on the best-selling game
by KONAMI®

Book created by F.X. Nine
Written by Christopher Howell
A Seth Godin Production

**This book is not authorized, sponsored, or endorsed
by Nintendo of America Inc.**

SCHOLASTIC INC.
New York Toronto London Auckland Sydney

This book is dedicated to Dave Bischoff

Special thanks to: Greg Holch, Jean Feiwel, Dick Krinsley, Dona Smith, Amy Berkower, Sheila Callahan, Nancy Smith, Joan Giurdanella, Henry Morrison, Michael Cader and especially Emil Heidkamp, Kay Wolf-Jones, and Kim Lee

No part of this publication may be reproduced in whole or in part, or stored in a retrieval system, or transmitted in any form or by any means, electronic, mechanical, photocopying, recording or otherwise, without written permission of the publisher. For information regarding permission, write to Scholastic Inc. 730 Broadway, New York, NY 10003

ISBN 0-590-43775-5

Copyright ©1990 by Seth Godin Productions, Inc. All rights reserved. Published by Scholastic Inc.
Simon's Quest® is a registered trademark of Konami Inc.
Konami® is a registered trademark of Konami Industry Co. Ltd.
WORLDS OF POWER™ is a trademark of Scholastic Inc.

12 11 10 9 8 7 6 5 4 3 2 1   0 1 2 3/9

Printed in the U.S.A.   01

First Scholastic printing, July 1990

CHAPTER ONE

Tim

It looked as though Count Dracula was going to win the battle.

"I will drink your spirit like cherry pop!" said the count, flapping his cape and showing his fangs. "Yes, Simon Belmont! You will become one of my children of the night!"

Simon shivered with fear.

They both stood upon a castle tower. Beyond was darkness, except for a cold moon in the sky like a dead eye. Wind chuckled softly along the battlements. The air was full of the smell of the garlic-clove necklace Simon had around his neck.

"No, Count Dracula! You will not drink my spirit this day!" he said, snapping his thorn whip with a crack as loud as a gunshot. "And by the way, it doesn't taste like cherry pop at all, so it's nothing you'd want anyway!"

"Let me be the judge of that!"

And the vampire leapt at him. He flapped his long arms and they became wings. His gigantic teeth gleamed as the mouth opened wide, seeking to bite!

"No you don't, Count Dracula," said Simon Belmont, his long blond hair streaming in the night wind. He held up the magical item he had worked so long and hard to obtain. "For I have the power of the Magic Crystal and that is the one —"

"Timothy!"

Simon Belmont started.

"Timothy Bradley! Are you listening to me?"

Simon dropped the Magic Crystal. It smashed to the floor and burst into a thousand brilliant pieces.

Count Dracula laughed cruelly. "Ah! A vampire has no better ally than a mother!"

He leapt on the boy, and then . . .

The magical world of Castlevania dissolved around Tim Bradley like twinkling gossamer. No longer was he Simon Belmont, vampire hunter. Once more he was in his boring bedroom. His mother stood in the doorway.

"Timothy! You've got school in less than ten minutes! How many times do I have to tell you, no Nintendo games in the morning! You get too wrapped up in them and you're late for your classes."

Tim put down the joystick. "Ah, gee, Mom. I almost got Count Dracula again!"

"Didn't you tell me that you already got the count?" Judy Bradley asked, bending her frown toward the TV set. She was a pretty woman, even with her dark brown hair in curlers. But she didn't look so hot when she frowned. "More than once, as I recall."

"Nineteen times!" said Tim proudly,

reaching up and turning off the TV set. "This would have been the twentieth."

"Well, just use your imagination to pretend the count got staked again and run along to school, chum."

Tim shook his head as he got up and began digging through a pile of comic books for his prized pair of black leather Reebok shoes. He found one of them and began to put it on.

"You just don't understand, Mom. I'll know I didn't win. That's what matters."

He dropped down and began to feel around under his bed for the other shoe. His hand encountered miniature model monsters and warriors, marbles, a slingshot, then finally came across the soft leather top of a tennis shoe.

"Well, mothers never do understand, I suppose," said Mrs. Bradley. "That's part of our job. I do understand, though, that if this happens once more your father's going to hear about this and *whoops!* There will go that allowance that keeps you nose-high in comic books!"

Tim slipped on the other shoe. Tied it. "Message received. Over and I'm outta here!"

He grabbed his books, and a half-eaten chocolate granola bar for breakfast, and ran past his mother and down the stairs, taking them two at a time. Although he was short and he wasn't exactly varsity sports material, Tim Bradley was quick. His friends wanted him to play pickup touch football all the time. He, however, was just as happy to exercise his finger and thumb in front of a video game. Like books, they were whole worlds he could get lost in, zooming with fighter planes or roving through adventures with deadly Ninjas.

Tim's favorite game, however, was Konami's Castlevania.

He had never gotten through Bram Stoker's famous novel *Dracula*. It was too darned scary. And Stephen King! Whew! Tim liked fantasy plenty, but when it came to horror books, horror films, or horror comic books Tim's knees just turned to water. This was why he liked Castlevania so much. He could deal with Dracula there. He felt like he had control.

Tim Bradley was a short fourteen-year-old who wore black horn-rimmed glasses just to be eccentric. He had dark hair and a narrow face, but it was an open and friendly face when he took off the spectacles.

Tim Bradley certainly didn't think he was good-looking. He just saw himself as being pretty average. Except at video games. At video games, he was a real champ.

As he ran to school, where he attended the eighth grade, he took a bite of his chocolate granola bar. This was one of his weaknesses. Not granola bars. Chocolate. If he could, he would have eaten a Hershey's Big Block for breakfast. Mom compromised by buying him chocolate granolas with healthy stuff like raisins and nuts.

"Too much chocolate is bad for your complexion, Tim," she'd say. "Besides, it puts on weight."

Tim had a clear complexion, and he was slim, so it was hard to understand what his mother was talking about. But since he still lived at home and would until he grew up (Boy, he couldn't wait to do that!) he had to do what his parents said, more or less. Anyway, he knew that chocolate wasn't good for you. He just loved it. Always had, and probably always would. Especially the gooey, rich fudge that his grandmother made that he would wash down with big glasses of cold foamy milk and — Gosh! Just thinking about it made him gobble up the rest of the breakfast bar.

If he had looked off to the right, behind a large clump of juniper bushes, he would have seen a famous hero from another dimension materializing with a quiet *pop*. As it happened, the famous hero had come specifically to speak to none other than Timothy J. Bradley.

However, the hero was so overcome by culture shock that he could only stare at the wonders about him, allowing Tim Bradley to be on his way to homeroom.

GAME HINT

There's a secret path at Yuba Lake.

CHAPTER TWO

Simon

"Hi, Tim," said the cutest girl in junior high to Tim Bradley. "Janet Morrison told me you could give me some good tips on where to get discount rates on video game cartridges. My brother's birthday is coming up and I need to buy him a nice present."

Blink of chocolate-brown eyes. A smile so brilliant it dazzled Tim's brain from cerebrum to cerebellum.

Wow! He'd always liked Carol Jance since he'd started here at Howard Junior High last year. And though they shared homeroom, and Carol was nice enough to acknowledge his existence, unlike other more socially conscious teenage females who shunned him, she'd never actually sought him out.

For advice yet!

Tim Bradley looked around him at the rest of the homeroom class, at the hand of the clock close to the eight-thirty bell.

How come everyone wasn't watching this momentous occasion? How come there weren't trumpets and firecrackers and streamers flying through the air like New Year's Eve?

"Uhm... well... Blockbuster Discount

has a real good sale on them now, actually." Carol sure smelled nice, too. He realized he'd never been this close to her before, and it was not an unpleasant experience. Tim Bradley didn't normally notice girls much. There were far more important things to be thinking about in his life. However, with her brunette good looks perking just inches from him, he certainly noticed Carol. And it was an experience with every bit the excitement of a nervous moment in the middle of the game Zelda.

"Oh, good!" she said. But then a small cloud dimmed her smile. "Oh, dear. I haven't the faintest idea where Blockbuster Discount is." She smiled glowingly again. "I don't suppose you'd be willing to take me there this afternoon, would you?"

"Uhm . . . er . . . sure. Sure, Carol. I'd be more than happy to take you there. It's not far away from school. I mean, it's so close that we could just walk!"

"Magnificent!" She grabbed his forearm and squeezed it with enthusiasm. "See you at the flagpole outside the main entrance at 3:15 P.M.! It's a date!" She gave his arm another squeeze and she was off in a flurry of skirt, fluffy blouse, swirling hair, and that wonderful flowery perfume.

A date?

A date with Carol Jance, eighth-grade beauty?

It all sounded okay to Tim Bradley. Especially since it involved video games. That was something he could talk about. He'd have problems with other stuff.

Still, it wasn't a date-date. Not like a movie at the mall or anything formal like that. It was just him and Carol, going to Blockbusters, looking for bargains. Right?

But the way his heart was beating, you would have thought she'd asked him to the junior prom.

The bell rang. Tim picked up his books, drifted out into the hallway through the flow of noisy teens elbowing and clomping toward first-period classes. The odor of chalk dust and floor wax filled the halls.

Tim was fantasizing about kicking through a hot game of Double Dragon, Carol Jance by his side, when he ran smack into Burt Alvin by the boys' room.

It was like running into a truck.

"Hey!" said the ninth-grader, frowning down on him from about twenty stories above. Tim peered up the heights from the level of Burt Alvin's chest to his chiseled features above. "Hey! Bradley!"

"Huh?"

"What's this about a date with my girl?"

"Date? Girl?"

"Yeah. You know. As in female. Pretty. Carol. Mine!" Each of the last four words was accompanied by a hard poke from a forefinger.

Uh-oh! Tim had forgotten. Carol had a boyfriend. A big boyfriend. Maybe she was getting ready to dump him, though. No matter. Tim was still dead meat if Donkey Kong here thought that he was trespassing on his territory.

"Oh. That. Uh...gee, Burt. She just wants me to take her shopping for video games."

"The video jockey wants to ride off in the sunset with my girl, huh? Well, pal, let me tell you...I'm perfectly capable of taking Carol to any store she wants to go to. But I tell you, I feel like putting you out of commission just for thinking about going out with my girl!"

What to do, what to do?

"Look, Burt. I was just headed into the boys' room. Can we discuss this when I'm finished?"

Burt glared at him. "Yeah. I guess so. Don't want you to have any accidents while I'm pulverizing you!"

"That's very thoughtful of you, Burt. Which reminds me of a funny joke I heard the other day." Tim Bradley loved jokes. He loved puns, too. And like he always said, the badder the better. "Why does the chicken cross the bathroom?"

"Move it, man. I'll be waitin' for you right here!"

Tim pushed through the swinging door. He went to a sink, ran cold water, and splashed his face.

Boy, oh, boy! Was he in trouble!

What was he going to do? The word around school was that the last kid who crossed Burt Alvin was wearing concrete braces at the bottom of Bulmer Pond.

Tim was pretty good when it came to wrestling Hulk Hogan or Macho Man on his Nintendo, but when it came to real life, he wasn't the kind of kid to fight much.

Gosh, he was really in kind of a jam, and it wasn't the grape kind, either.

"Excuse me," said a deep voice from behind him. "Are you Timothy Bradley?"

Tim jumped. Startled, he looked up into the mirror.

Standing behind him was a tall, blond-haired man who looked like a superhero from a comic book only with short hair and a vulnerable, perplexed look on his face. But boy, his costume sure wasn't anything from this century! He wore what looked like hand-made sheep's wool jacket and trousers with a sackcloth shirt cinched at the waist by a wide leather belt. His black boots were leather as well. He smelled distinctly of garlic.

"Yes. That's me. What is this, Halloween already?"

"May I introduce myself." Tim noted a distinct accent. "I am Simon Belmont. I have come here to your dimension to seek your help with a dreadfully important quest. The fate of Castlevania — to say nothing of my soul, my life, and the soul and life of the woman I love — are at stake!"

"Oh," said Tim. "And I thought I had problems."

CHAPTER THREE

The Return of Dracula—Sort of

Right.

Here was Simon Belmont, the Hero of Castlevania, standing before him, square jaw jutting earnestly, broad chest heaving with purpose. Yes, this was Simon all right. Tim even noticed now that gripped feverishly in Simon's fist was a whip. Around his neck on a leather thong was a beautiful golden ring that shone and glittered like the heart of a sun.

"Righteous, dude," said a long-haired guy with leather pants, just coming into the boys' room. "Aren't you Metallica or somethin'!"

"No," said Simon, eyes flashing with dark earnestness. "I'm from Castlevania!"

"Great group, man! Got all your CD's!" The guy cruised out of the boys' room thrashing power chords on his heavy-metal air guitar.

Simon looked quizzically at Tim.

"If you don't know, don't ask," said Tim. "Look—anyway, this is a joke, right? Everyone has ganged up on me 'cause they know I'm an ace Castlevania player and I'm being persecuted for my hobby."

"No! I swear, upon my sacred honor!" insisted Simon.

"Sure. Okay, suppose there really is a Castlevania, and you really are Simon Belmont. What's your girlfriend's name, huh? Answer me that?"

"Why, Linda Entwhistle, of course."

"Hmm. You've done your research. Okay, tell me then, Mr. Simon Belmont. Why do you want me to help you?"

"Why? Because you are the best Castlevania player in this dimension. Because this Holy Ring bestowed upon myself by none other than the beauteous Linda Entwhistle guided me to you to sincerely seek your aid."

"Against who?"

"Why, Dracula, of course."

"You see! You can't be Simon Belmont! You, I mean, I — defeat that crummy old vampire all the time!"

"There is no time for an explanation! You must come with me immediately. I entreat you, Timothy Bradley! Please!"

"I don't know . . . I —"

Suddenly there was a loud pounding on the boys' room door. "Hey, Bradley. Come on out of there and get what you deserve."

"Say. If you're Simon Belmont how'd you get here?"

"Why through an interdimensional doorway, of course, created by this magical ring."

"Show me . . . get me out of here, and I'll believe you."

"Where would you like to go?"

"Home!"

"Come. Grab my whip, Timothy Bradley."

Well, it was worth a shot, thought Tim. Anything to get away from that walking dynamite truck with biceps. At the very least, he'd give this a try and if it didn't work, he could get muscle brain here to use his whip on Burt.

He reached out and grabbed the leather whip.

It felt as though he'd grabbed a live wire.

"*Yow!*" he said. He felt his hair stand on end. Energy coursed full throttle through his body. A burst of light zapped through his eyes. Then everything became a pleasant calm after the silent bang.

"You really shouldn't play around with shocks," he told Simon. "You could electrocute a guy. There's this guy outside I'd like you to — Huh?!"

The "huh" was because he'd just realized that he and Simon Belmont were no longer in the junior high school boys' room.

They stood in his bedroom, back at home.

"This is where you live, is it not, Timothy Bradley?"

"Yeah! *Wow!* So it is." He turned newly admiring eyes toward the hero. "You really are Simon Belmont!"

"You acknowledge my identity. Thank you. Does that mean that you are now willing to come back with me to my homeland to rescue it from the power of darkness, the disease called Dracula?"

"Dracula. Right. I thought the old popsicle sucker was dead!"

"Oh, indeed. Very dead. His body has been cut up and it has been placed in five different places."

"Sounds pretty dead to me, Simon. What's the problem then?"

"His curse. It spreads across my homeland. I should have burned the body and scattered the ashes to the four winds! His followers have separated his body parts and hidden them! I don't know what to do! And Linda Entwhistle has been snatched away from me! She came to me in a vision and gave me this ring and —"

"Whoa! One thing at a time, puh-lease," said Tim. "I'm a boy of my word, Simon. I'll come with you, but I've got to pack a few important items first."

Tim began jamming stuff into an empty laundry bag. Stuff he was going to need. Like chocolate bars. A Swiss army knife. Chocolate M&M's. A sweater. Some more Hershey's Chocolate Bars (semi-sweet, milk, Mr. Goodbar and gosh, don't forget the one with almonds). His Boy Scout kit including compass and campfire starter. Some Reese's Pieces. (Hey, if Simon Belmont really existed, maybe he could lure E.T. down from the skies, too!) Some clean underwear.

And, last of all, his very best imported

Godiva chocolates, for emergencies, celebrations, or just for the heck of it.

"What is all that?" inquired Simon Belmont.

"Chocolate. About my favorite thing in the world, except maybe for bad jokes, puns, and — oh yeah — video games."

"Chocolate? We have no such thing in Castlevania!"

"It's a good thing I'm bringing a supply then, Simon. It's candy."

"Oh, yes. Candy. Very bad for your teeth, though."

"You know, you're a pretty serious guy, aren't you!"

"I think, Timothy Bradley, you'd be pretty serious, too, if you had only forty-eight hours to prevent your body from being totally possessed by the evil spirit of Count Dracula himself!"

A voice from below interrupted them. "Timothy! Is that you? I hear voices up there!"

"*Oops!*" Tim gasped, really frightened now. "That's my mom!"

"Are 'moms' a form of evil demon here on this plane?" said Simon Belmont, spinning about and grabbing his whip, ready for battle.

"Uh-huh. Worse. Can we just take off for Castlevania now before I really get into trouble!"

Footsteps sounded on the stairs.

"Timothy! When your father hears about

this, it's going to be no video games for a month! That should do the trick!"

The footsteps were on the landing now, coming closer, closer, like claps of doom.

Tim Bradley grabbed the whip.

"I think that dealing with Dracula is going to be a vacation."

"I think not!" said Simon Belmont.

Again the shock, the feeling of being uprooted and thrown into a pool of dazzle. Shapes and smells and colors swirled in on him like angry ghosts. A chill bit through his shirt, making him glad that he had brought along a sweater in his sack. Then darkness clutched around him like a fist.

"Where are we?" Tim asked when they had seemed to come to a stop.

"Welcome," said Simon Belmont, "to Castlevania!"

GAME HINT

Take the top path
in the Veros Woods
to get to Berkeley Mansion.

CHAPTER FOUR

Castlevania Caper

Castlevania, of course, was a name that Tim Bradley always figured came from "Castle" and "Transylvania." The place that Simon Belmont called Castlevania, however, looked nothing like Tim imagined it might from the names alone. Certainly, he could see stone castles. Certainly, the place held all the menace implied by Transylvania, the birthplace for the legend of vampires.

However, otherwise it was quite a surprise.

"Golly, Simon! Things are pretty creepy here in Castlevania at night, huh?"

Simon Belmont lifted an eyebrow. "Creepy? Yes, certainly. But it's not night here now, Timothy. It's broad daylight!"

Tim Bradley took a double take. "Day! But that's the moon up there, isn't it?"

"No, Timothy. That's the sun. Since the curse of Dracula came upon this dimension, a shadow has been cast over my land and a chill has touched its heart."

Tim shivered. "Boy, I'll say. I mean, take a look at this place!

And what a place it was. Castlevania looked like a cluster of medieval towns, but drawn by a madman in a depression, and inked with about a thousand colored shades of dark. Buildings slanted dangerously, towers leaned further than the Tower of Pisa. The thatched-roof houses looked like they'd been left in the sun too long and then quick-frozen. The place smelled foresty, but a forest filled with mold, fungus, and mildew. The single bright aspect was the taste of gingerbread in the air.

It made Tim hungry enough to take out a Hershey bar and start chewing. The candy boosted his spirits.

"So anyway, here we are," he said between bites. "We won't have to worry about Burt or my mom in Castlevania. You want to tell me the rest of the story?"

Simon Belmont nodded gravely.

"When I killed Dracula, after all that struggle — "

"Boy, you bet it's a struggle! It took me a whole two months to win my first game! And I thought my thumbs were going to fall off!"

Simon frowned and put his hands on his hips. "Please. You are going to have to keep a little quiet so that I may relate my story!"

"Oh. Yeah. Sorry about that."

"After all that struggle, after I defeated Dracula, I did not realize that I should have burned his body and then scattered the ashes. No, I thought I had won the day, and so I left him with the stake in his heart. I knew something was wrong when my beautiful Linda, whom Dracula had captured, did not come back to me!" Simon put a hand over his heart, lowered his head, and sighed.

A pang nudged Tim. Gee, he felt really sorry for this guy. After all that effort, he doesn't get the love of his life back. It was at this moment that Tim Bradley determined that Yes! He would do his very best to help Simon Belmont. This was a good man.

"That's okay, Simon," said Tim. "We'll get her back! Together. Even though this is the weirdest looking place I've ever seen, and I'm not really sure if this is a dream."

"Oh, make no mistake, this is no dream. Dracula is very real. And his power is far more than I thought it was. When I left his body in his coffin, his helpers came. They cut Dracula in five parts."

"His evil soul swept throughout the dimension, a temporary stay from its banishment. For you see, Timothy Bradley, the soul of Dracula has forty-eight hours to find a body to possess so that it can remain here!"

Like bad movie music, a wind swept through some nearby trees snatching off the last of the leaves and rattling the limbs. A shiver of dread went up Tim Bradley's spine. *Yikes!* he realized. This was no Halloween prank. This felt like the real thing!

"You mean — like me!"

Simon Belmont turned a haunted look toward Tim. "No. Me!"

"You? Why would he want you!"

"He must possess the last person he infected with his blood," said the hero. He unrolled his sleeve. On his arm were three parallel grooves, filled with scabbed blood. "The scars of Dracula, Timothy Bradley. I am the person he must possess. And this is the true problem. This is why I need an aide to help me through Castlevania. This is why I need your help so desperately."

"You mean, if he takes you over, you'll become a vampire!"

"Yes. And then, the monster shall again rule my beloved home of Castlevania!"

True dread jolted Tim Bradley.

He felt the intense need for a Hershey's Big Block come over him. But where was his pack? Oh, yes — he bent over and rummaged though its contents with his hand.

"Sounds pretty serious, Simon. You're saying you've got two days to stop Dracula. I suppose that means you have to find those body parts, right? You put him together, you fight him again, you beat him again, and this time you destroy him forever!" He found the chocolate bar and gripped it. "Hey, you know, this would make a fantastic video game!" He turned back around, starting to tear the wrapping off the candy bar. "In fact, when I get back, I'm going to write to a game company immediately and suggest that — *Yikes!*"

The "yikes!" was said in good cause.

For Simon Belmont was no longer totally Simon Belmont.

"Greetings, mortal!" said the voice of Count Dracula. "Come to Castlevania for an early and unpleasant death, I take it?"

Tim Bradley dropped his candy bar.

CHAPTER FIVE

Dr. Simon and Mr. Dracula

Simon Belmont was undergoing a transformation like nothing Tim Bradley had ever seen before.

His back was bending over like a hunchback's and his fingers grew hairy. His nose lengthened and tapered to a point, his face thinning, his mouth drawing into a cruel sneer.

The hair became limp and greasy. It was like Dr. Jekyll turning into Mr. Hyde — only much, much worse!

And the eyes!

The eyes became narrow slits behind which pupils glowed like live coals in a furnace. They burned through Tim like laser beams edged with razor blades.

If Tim Bradley could have screamed, he would have let out a long, loud one. Unfortunately, he was so paralyzed with fear that he could barely move, let alone make a sound. Dracula was taking over Simon Belmont's body!

"Ah-ha! You are a puny little nothing, aren't you? Why ever did Simon Belmont choose you?" asked Dracula's voice, coming from Simon's transformed body. "I can see that my success in taking over his body is virtually assured!"

"Oh, yeah!" Tim blurted, breaking out of his freeze. "I happen to have already beaten you nineteen times!"

"Is that right, mortal? I certainly remember none of those times. You are a silly thing, aren't you. I shall enjoy hearing you squeal and feeling you squirm when I sink my lovely fangs into your soul!"

"Is that the tooth?" Tim shot back.

"Arrgh!" cried Dracula's voice. Simon's body jerked back as though physically struck. "A pun! I abhor puns! If there's anything I can't stand more, it's stupid, silly jokes!"

"Really! Well then, Drac, maybe you'd know why a duck flies looking down?"

"No!" Simon's body shook with violent tremors. "No! Stop or I shall tear you to pieces!"

"Because he doesn't want to quack up!"

"Arrggghhhhhh!" The vampire's face now seemed to be merely superimposed over that of Simon Belmont's. And that double-imaged face was freaking out! "Dumb joke! Stupid joke!"

"No, Drac," said Tim Bradley, sensing victory within his grasp. "It's a fowl joke!"

The vampire's face contorted with outrage. His eyes bugged so wide, they appeared as though they were going to pop out. *"Baahhhhhhhhhhhhh!"* he said. "I shall revenge myself upon you for that, mortal! Take

22

heed. Your blood and your soul will belong to me!"

"Don't Count Dracula your chickens before they're hatched, wimp-pire!"

Dracula didn't even get a scream out for that one. The fanged mouth just opened incredibly wide, and then *pop!* the flattened picture of the count imploded, leaving Simon back the way he'd originally been. Only looking more pained, if that was possible.

"That was the very worst yet!" he said. "The accursed vampire almost had me then. If not for you and your jokes, my new friend, I surely would have fallen under his sway!"

"Hey, give yourself some credit. You put some willpower into the battle, I'm sure," said Tim. He was feeling braver already. That old fool wasn't such a danger after all! Ha, ha! This would be just like an easy video game!

"You realize that now Count Dracula will be after your body and soul as well!"

Tim shrugged nonchalantly. "I can handle it."

"If he defeats me and gains the use of my body and remains in this dimension, he will take great pleasure in flaying every inch of your skin off!"

Tim blinked.

"And after he pours salt on your raw nerves, he will dip you into a vat of acid!"

Tim gulped.

"And then, Timothy Bradley, he will start torturing you!"

"Uh, Simon. You know, I think I'm going to need more chocolate for this little expedition. And, uh, I just remember, I'm allergic to garlic. Maybe you'd better get my older brother Fred. He's really much better than I am at Castlevania!"

However, Simon Belmont had already spun on his heel and had started down the road.

"Come, Timothy Bradley. We shall go to the local tavern where we shall get our supplies and plan our strategy!"

Tim Bradley stood still for a moment, trying to figure a way out of this business.

But then the darkness closed in, cold and ominous.

He grabbed his bag of necessities and tripped on down the cobblestones after the blond hero.

CHAPTER SIX

The Seven Deadly Sins

Tim Bradley took a drink of the hot cocoa he'd mixed over the hearth fire of the Hart and Sole Tavern.

"So, what now, Simon?" he said, leaning back into the chair, feeling much better here in the soft shadows of this comfortable inn. The chubby red-nosed innkeeper, a fellow by the name of Pedersen, had treated them to a filling meal of cheese, bread, and fruit. He'd also packed a nice backpack for Simon as well. Doubtless, they would get hungry during their quest. And even Tim had to admit he couldn't live on chocolate alone.

"Now, we rest," said Simon, munching on an apple. "We rest and we wait until nightfall!"

Tim spluttered on his milk. "What?! Wait until nightfall! I mean, isn't it dark enough? Can't we start, like tomorrow morning when that joke of a sun comes back out?"

Simon shook his head. "First, we need rest, but not that much rest. Second, we need energy!"

"Have a chocolate bar!"

"No, not that sort of energy, Timothy. Magical energy. For you see, at night wraithghouls emerge from their damp holes." He held up his thorn whip. "Linda has told me that if I dispatch them with this whip into the dimension from which they came, they will leave behind the energy that animates them. And I—and you—will be able to absorb that energy."

"Ghouls, huh?" Tim shuddered. "So then, what's next after that?"

"You simply follow me. I have been given some clues as to the locations of the body pieces of Dracula. However, we must obtain other magical items to aid us on our quest, along with assistance from the townspeople, priests, and others. However, we must be very careful—for the power of Dracula is such that these people may tell us lies. Somehow we must verify their truth or untruth. Perhaps me might find a magical tool to allow us to do so."

"We bump around in the dark, asking directions?" Tim asked, a distinct uneasiness inside him.

"If you like, we may leave now and take what we can of the light. However, in order to get the *dimensional* energy we need, we shall have to hunt for monsters in the outlying woods beyond."

"Never mind," said Tim. "I guess I'll take my chances tonight." He tried to cheer up. "Hey, should we bring diamonds?"

"Diamonds? Why diamonds?"

"Because, don't they say, 'Diamonds are a ghoul's best friend'?"

Simon Belmont looked at Tim as though

he were from another planet. Which he was, of course. Well, another dimension anyway.

Tim could see that Simon was the deadly serious type who didn't get jokes. It didn't matter. The dude was big and the dude was brave, and he meant well.

"Gee," said Tim, laughing. "At least Dracula gets my jokes. He doesn't like them much, but he gets them."

Simon shrugged and proceeded with his instructions.

"What you witnessed back on the street was my worst attack yet. Dracula is attempting to control me. However, usually he works in the traditional ways — like temptation. You see, we all have dark sides, Timothy Bradley. We are all mixtures of good and evil. Yes, even I, Simon Belmont, hero of Castlevania. It is through this avenue, this dark side, that the spirit of Dracula generally sneaks up on me. This is one of the reasons I need you. To help me fight him off. Not only in the manner you used before, but by pointing out to me the telltale signs by my behavior."

"You mean, like if you start kicking old ladies."

Simon's eyebrows knitted with bafflement, but then understanding dawned on him. He did not, however, smile at the exaggeration. "Ah. Yes. I see. No, I do not normally kick old ladies. This would be a sin. In fact, if I begin to show signs of committing any of the seven deadly sins, warn me!"

"The seven deadly sins. Let me see. What are those? Ah, yes... Gluttony. That's one." Tim took a big mouthful of his cheese sandwich and then dug into his sack for a chocolate bar. "Lethargy." Tim yawned. "You know, I could use a little sleep."

"Beware, Timothy Bradley! Count Dracula could well be tempting you!"

Tim blinked, but then waved off the notion. "What? 'Cause I'm hungry and a little tired?"

Simon nodded. "Perhaps you are right. In any event, the other deadly sins are deceit, jealousy, lust, anger, and blasphemy. If you see any of them creeping into my actions or words, you should . . . you should — "

"Hit you over the head with a sledgehammer?"

"No. No, that would hurt me too much."

"Hey! It's a joke! Don't you Castlevanians have jokes?"

"Of course we do, Timothy! We are not Zombies!" Simon cleared his throat. "How many vampires does it take to light a lantern?"

"Hey! Wow, great. A joke! Kind of like a lightbulb joke. I give up. What's the answer?"

Simon Belmont scratched his head. "I seem to have forgotten it. No matter. Not important. What is important, vitally important, is our mission."

Wow, thought Tim. Vampires, ghouls, monsters! The seven deadly sins, a quest, danger lurking in every mildewed corner!

This was not going to be your average Tim Bradley night of chocolate, popcorn, video games, chocolate, comic books, and more chocolate!

This was going to be one righteous adventure.

CHAPTER SEVEN

Ghouls Just Want To Have Fun

Simon Belmont snapped his whip.

Cr-rack!

The end of the whip hit the ghoul right in the misty stuff that composed its chest. The thing was hurled back a footstep, but then it righted itself and just kept on coming.

Simon pulled the whip back, readying it to crack again.

Tim Bradley just stood in his tracks, frightened out of his mind. This wasn't just any two-dimensional programmed TV image dot array that could be handled with a joystick. This was a living, breathing so-rotten-it-smelled-worse-than-Tim's-socks monster.

No, scratch that.

This was a dead, living, breathing monster.

The thing was about seven feet tall. Its gray skin hung down in tatters, revealing bones and worms beneath. Its popping orbs looked like the eyes of a long-dead fish. But when you looked closer at the grim thing, it got worse. When you looked closer, you saw that the thing was only half-solid. It seemed to be composed half of flesh and half of gray smog lit from within by an unearthly glow.

Simon's whip unfurled, catching the thing again, this time squarely in its skull face.

Cr-rack!

This time the whip had instant effect. An explosion like an M-80 going off in a garbage can sounded out. Shivers of energy-infested ectoplasm radiated around the whip's end. The whole creature shook. Then, with a bright shimmer, it seemed to wrench away from existence, as though some kind of hook had come out of nowhere and dragged it into a black hole, leaving only its outline behind.

The outline turned to a dazzle that glittered over Simon Belmont like faerie dust. Simon shivered, and his eyes got wide for a moment...

And then he recoiled his whip around his hand and nodded toward Tim. "Ah, yes. Energy! Already I feel recharged with vigor! I am ready for another!"

"Well, good for you, Simon. Me, I'm ready to go back to that safe, warm tavern!"

Tim wasn't serious. He knew that he had a job ahead of him that he had promised to do, and he wasn't the sort to weasel out of his commitments. But all in all, he would rather be back in the tavern, sipping hot chocolate than fighting ghouls in the middle of a dark Castlevanian night.

They'd finished their dinner back at the Hart and Sole. The innkeeper had wanted them to eat more, but Simon had insisted that too much to eat and drink would make them tired and heavy for tonight's action. Just a little catnap would do, he insisted.

And that was just what they'd had, too. A catnap. Right there on one of the benches of the Tavern, right beside two tavern cats. Fortunately, Tim's allergies weren't acting up, so he actually managed to go to sleep despite all the excitement of the day, and all the excitement yet to come, and all the caffeine in all the chocolate bars he'd devoured.

It must have been all that warm milk he'd drunk.

When he'd woken up, it was dark outside so he figured it was time to go. However, the "sun" was still up, even though it was low in the sky. They spent the remaining minutes warming up their muscles with exercises. Then Simon had prepared himself by sitting very still with his legs folded under him.

Tim had prepared himself by eating a bag of M&M's.

Simon's voice brought him back to the present.

"There is no time for loafing in warm taverns, Timothy Bradley. Look! Here come two more ghouls. You take one, while I deal with the other."

Sure enough, coming out of a narrow alley like two gravestones with arms, legs, and bad attitudes shambled two ghouls. They hissed harshly, opening mouths filled with sharp teeth. Long claws reached out to rend and tear at their victims.

All in all, it was not a pleasant sight.

Tim Bradley lifted the sword that Simon had given him just after they'd arrived at the inn.

He would have prefered a gun. However, Simon Belmont had informed him not only of the fact that there were no guns in Castlevania, but that even if they were imported from another dimension, they wouldn't work here. Gunpowder didn't explode in Castlevania. "Things work on magical principles here, Timothy," Simon had explained. "And also on the moral laws of good and evil. This is why I am very good, and Dracula is very bad."

Anyway, now Tim Bradley didn't have time to worry about the niceties of ethics and moral philosophy.

He had a snarling creature to deal with!

The ghoul bore down on him with surprising speed for something that looked like it was going to fall apart at any moment. Tim swung the sword over his head toward the creature, but somehow missed. The metal sword crashed down on the cobbles noisily. *Cr-rack!* sang the song of Simon's whip from behind him as the hero dealt with his ghoul.

The ghoul's razor-sharp fingernails reached out and ripped at Tim's jacket. The whole arm was torn!

"*Yow!*" said Tim. "My mom's gonna kill me!"

The ghoul just snarled and pushed its outstretched hands toward Tim Bradley's throat.

"You rat! I hope you have a mom, 'cause that's who I'm sending you back to!" With all his might, Tim lifted the sword and swung it toward the spot where Simon's whip had been so effective on the last ghoul. The thick, pitted blade sliced into the mist-skin, and immediately sparks flew like a blowout in a spiral galaxy.

As he watched with astonishment, the ghoul slowly faded away.

Before it was completely invisible, it was yanked from its existence on this plane, leaving behind only its outline. This outline hovered, shimmering, for an instant. And then, like a tiny piece cut from a whirlwind of light, it flew up the metal of Tim's sword.

It felt as though he'd stuck both hands into an electrical outlet. Energy coursed through him, but without a buzz, and it felt like his hair was standing on end.

He also felt as though he'd been jolted awake.

"Goodness!" he said, blinking as he turned to Simon. "That really packs a wallop!" He felt as though he'd just run a mile and then drunk a quart of Gatorade. Refreshed, vital, alert. "I feel like somebody just changed my batteries!"

"Yes, you see. Now we have sufficient energy to deal with the next part of our mission."

"Which is, pray tell?" asked Tim, fairly bouncing on the balls of his feet.

"According to Linda Entwhistle, first we must locate the rib of Dracula."

"That must be his funny bone. He sure seems to have lost it!" Gosh he felt alive and buoyant. He felt like he could conquer the world and then play two hours of touch football in the evening.

"Yes, perhaps. She said that we would receive a clue as to its whereabouts from the central signpost in the middle of Castlevania." Simon's face twitched. "First, though, I seem to be hungry again. Perhaps we should go back to the Hart and Sole Tavern. There we can eat a decent meal. Eggs and flapjacks, I should think. Oh, yes, and cake with whipped cream. And apples, lots of apples. And you can eat your chocolate and then we can wash it all down with yards of foamy ginger ale. And then we can eat sausages and jams and then perhaps we can think about dessert!"

This sounded good to Tim. He was always hungry. He could do with a couple of Cadbury bars, if only to celebrate his victory over the ghoul.

But then he caught himself up short.

This was the sort of warning sign that Simon had told him about. Wasn't gluttony one of the seven deadlies?

His stomach rumbled. Still, some pancakes would be awfully delicious.

"No!" he told himself. This was why he

was here. To help Simon resist temptations, not fall to them himself. He had a responsibility to fulfill, and he meant to do just that.

He kicked Simon Belmont in the butt. Not real hard, but firmly enough to wrest his attention away from treats and sweets. "Ouch!" said Simon. He lifted his whip up, turning a look of anger and menace on Tim. "Why do you strike me, mortal?"

"You see, you're even starting to sound like Dracula."

Simon's mouth dropped open. "Yes. You're right. And so you kicked me upon my nether parts." Simon patted Tim upon his shoulder. "Excellent! Already Linda has guided me truly in selecting such a fine fellow as you!"

Tim felt a stirring of feeling. He really liked this guy. When Simon Belmont had a good thought about someone, he shared it. He was thoughtful, sincere, and honest. So what if he was a bit unhip. He had his own brand of cool.

"Anytime, Simon!" Tim looked down the intersecting streets, deserted now, all wrapped in night and eerie mist. "Well, we'd better be going to that signpost now, right? The question is, which way?"

"Right, my true friend. The way to the signpost is no problem. Follow me!"

And Tim, trusting Simon to show him the correct way, followed.

CHAPTER EIGHT

The Signpost

"Good grief!" said Tim Bradley, gazing upon the thing with a mixture of awe and bafflement. "This is the weirdest signpost I've ever seen!"

"As I said, Timothy Bradley, things are not the same here in Castlevania as they are in your dimension!"

"Boy, I'll say!"

The sign was normal around the edges. Its stand was of wood — solid oak, from the looks of it. And the frame was wood as well.

However, it was the image inside the frame that was weird.

"Clouds," said Tim. "It looks like just a muddle of clouds. I feel like I'm looking into the Twilight Zone." He looked over his shoulder. "Is Rod Serling hiding anywhere around here by the way?"

"Twilight Zone?"

"Cultural reference. But what good is it going to do in getting our directions to Dracula's chest bone?"

"Just a moment, my friend. Observe!" From around his neck, Simon took the leather thong to which was tied the magical ring that had brought him to Earth and to Tim.

He picked the ring up between his fingers, and it sparkled with his touch.

Tim found himself holding his breath with excitement. There was something righteous and glorious about that ring now as Simon held it forth to the sign.

The gold and glitter touched the wood.

Tim Bradley gasped with wonder.

The clouds exploded with light.

Tim had to hold up his hand to shield his eyes. There was violet light, red light. Light of rainbow dazzle...

And then the light faded into a soft and simple radiance surrounding a face.

It was a woman's face, and it was the most beautiful woman that Tim Bradley had ever seen. She had eyes the color of the sky at its most blue and hair the color of honey. Her skin was soft and pure and clean. She was smiling, but it was a smile of sadness, of melancholy.

"Linda!" said Simon Belmont. "My wonderful and beautiful Linda Entwhistle! You were correct. At night, the signs can become portals into the dimension where you are imprisoned."

Linda Entwhistle smiled understandingly at her beloved. "I should think that's fairly obvious, darling. But, ah! I see that you have successfully brought the hero from Earth here. And my goodness, he is a handsome young man!"

Tim blushed. "Hi!" was all he could manage.

"He has already saved me from Dracula twice," said Simon. "But time grows short, Linda. We must seek out the five vital parts of Dracula you have described. The closest, you say, is Dracula's rib. But where is this rib?"

Linda Entwhistle's image shook and quivered as though the sign were a magical television screen and something were interfering with the transmission.

"There are limits to the power of the ring you hold, my darling," she said. "It, too, is affected by the curse of Dracula upon the land of Castlevania. When I attempt to tell you the direct truth of the locations of these parts of Dracula, the message is garbled. Therefore, I must tell you indirectly, through puzzles and riddles."

"Puzzles and riddles?" said Simon, cringing. "I am not too good with puzzles and riddles, Linda. You know that!"

"Yes, my dear. I remember how baffled you were when we played such games as children. However, this is one of the reasons I had you seek the help of Tim Bradley here. Tim, you are good with such brain teasers, are you not?"

"Well, that's what my teachers say, and I do like to do crosswords and stuff sometimes. But I'm not really the best. I don't know why you chose me."

She smiled. "Perhaps for your modesty. Now there are people . . . "

A kind of static frizzed through the

"screen" shot with veins of blood red.

"... different. These will also be told in puzzles and riddles."

"Stop," said Simon. "We didn't get the last part. There was an interruption."

Linda Entwhistle cleared her throat. "I said, there are people of Castlevania and the surrounding environs who have learned of the whereabouts of these pieces of Dracula."

"And they know the how-abouts to get to them."

"Precisely. You are a sharp fellow, young Tim!" She sent him a smile. Tim's pulse quickened. *Wow!* Forget Carol Jance back home! A guy could really fall hard for a lady like Linda Entwhistle. Tim could feel a stupendous crush squeezing in on him hard already!

"Ah, yes! Of course!" said Simon. "All good Castlevanians would want to rid this land of Dracula!"

"All good people everywhere would want to get rid of a vampire, Simon," Linda admonished. "However, to protect themselves, these people must deliver their messages in riddles and puzzles as well."

"Understood, understood," said Simon impatiently. "Much as I adore you, Linda, we really need to find out the location of that rib!"

"What you need can be found," said Linda Entwhistle, "where love is joined and Sundays sound."

And then, with a flash of colored smoke,

the image of Linda's face swept away, re- placed by the previous clouds.

" 'Where love is joined and Sundays sound,' " said Simon scratching. "Well now, that doesn't make much sense, Linda! Love isn't a thing so how can it be joined? And days don't make any sounds as far as I know!"

All Tim could think was that he was glad this guy had a lot of goodness, bravery, and muscle, because he sure didn't have much in the way of brains.

"She wants us to go to a church, Simon! Love is joined by marriage, usually in a church," he said. "Are there any churches close by?"

"Well, actually there's only one church in Castlevania . . . so I guess that must be the one she wants us to go to."

"Let's just get to that church before any more of those weird ghouls show up. I en- joyed the energy boost, but I might not be as lucky next time with this sword."

"Perhaps we can get you another weap- on. At least you'll have a choice, if need be."

They started off, Tim looking wistfully back behind them at the signpost where Lin- da Entwhistle's face had been.

CHAPTER NINE

The Church

The only church in Castlevania proved to be not only the old-fashioned European cathedral type, but a mighty big one, more than big enough, according to Simon, to fit all of Castlevania's citizens inside.

"This way!" said Simon, gesturing impatiently for Tim to hurry. His footsteps echoed as he entered.

The inside was lit by candles. Candles, candles, everywhere! More candles, it seemed, than on a thousand birthday cakes combined. Up ahead, Tim could see Simon walking down an aisle. The place smelled of candle wax and age, and it all seemed ancient and holy.

Tim hurried along to catch up with his friend. The echoes of his own footsteps skitted along the floor excitedly, without the sound of authority of his friend's.

"Wait up!" he called to the hero, and his voice came back to him from the walls like a choir.

However, despite his call, Simon was intent upon his goal: the altar. When Simon reached it, he took the handle of his whip and knocked on the wood three times.

Almost immediately, a man wearing a

gray hooded robe stepped out from the alcove. He walked up to Simon.

"Yes, my son."

"I am on a quest, Brother. I seek to rid this land of the curse of Dracula."

Tim walked up, and opened his mouth to make a quip.

However, something stilled him. There was something about this place, but especially about this holy man that said, "No jokes, please."

The monk looked at Simon, and then over to Tim. "The monster's evil even penetrates the walls of this church."

"Yes. You can help us though?"

"Indeed, I shall do what I can," the monk said solemnly. His hand reached back, and he took off his hood. His eyes fairly sparkled with good humor — but the frown on his face showed he knew well how serious the situation was.

"We are having a white elephant sale of certain items to benefit charity. Have you sufficient coin that you can buy these things?"

"Oh!" said Tim. "Simon, this must be part of what Linda was talking about. He wants to pass these things along in an indirect manner." Tim rummaged through his pockets and came up with two quarters, a dime, three nickels, and a penny. But by the time he put out his hand to offer the coins, Simon was already tinkling three gold pieces into the outstretched palm of the monk.

"Thank you, Brother Simon." The man turned and retrieved a wooden box from the altar behind him. "Your items of purchase are enclosed." The monk handed Simon the box and began to walk away back into the cloisters of the church.

"Hey, wait!" called Tim. "What about the puzzle I'm supposed to solve about the next part of our journey?"

The monk turned around and gazed at Tim quizzically. "Oh, you mean the part about where to find Dracula's rib?"

Tim was astounded. *"Shhhhhh!"* he said. "This is all supposed to be hush-hush!"

"The rib, my friend, would be at Berkeley Mansion! You just leave to the right from here—" he gestured — "and take Bulgaria Road straight on into Jova Woods. Now, be forewarned. The paths are very confusing there, but I'm sure you'll muddle through."

Tim's mouth had dropped. "But . . . but what about . . . I mean, Dracula might hear you!"

The monk shrugged. "I'll take my chances."

With that, the monk left them.

"Well, there's a brave fellow for you," said Simon. "Now let's see what we've got here in this box, shall we?" He set it down onto a pew and opened the lid.

Tim was still overwhelmed by the monk. *"Wow!* What a guy! Too bad the rest of the Castlevanians aren't as brave as he is!"

"The rest of the Castlevanians don't

have the trappings of a church to protect them. They're out in the middle of all that darkness!" Simon pulled out a large flask. "Excellent! Look what we have here, Tim!"

"Great. A canteen of water!" said Tim sarcastically.

"Ah, but not just any water," said Simon, holding the flask reverently. "Holy water."

"Well that's all very well and good, but what does it do?"

Simon seemed baffled by that one. "We shall just have to find out, won't we?"

"What else?"

Simon retrieved two whips. Tim recognized them immediately. They were thorn whips. Long, beautifully crafted thorn whips.

"Excellent!" said Simon. "The battles with the ghouls damaged my other whip. Now I have a new one. And you have another weapon, if you care to use it."

"Well, I suppose I could try," said Tim. "Still, I'm getting pretty good with this sword, huh?"

Simon said nothing.

"Okay, okay, but I am getting better, aren't I?"

Simon raised an eyebrow.

Tim held out his hand. "Just how do you snap one of these babies, anyway?"

Tim gave him the whip.

"It just takes practice, Timothy. Practice. You keep on doing it and that's the way you do it correctly. This is one of the lessons that your video games have taught you, is it not? Could you win the games when you first tried them?"

"Nope. But this is different. They were fun!"

Simon looked his friend right in the eye. "All of life is not fun, Timothy Bradley. If you learn nothing else from this adventure, then you should learn that. So what else do we have here?"

Simon reached in, grabbed something, and lifted it out.

At first, Tim thought it was a diamond. And if it was a diamond, it was the biggest that Tim had ever seen.

But then he saw it wasn't a diamond. Although it was mostly white, it had streaks of red in it. Tim had never seen anything at all like that in a diamond.

"It's some sort of crystal," he said in wonder even as it sparkled and shone like a fireworks display.

"Yes," said Simon. "And if my hunch is correct, then not only is it a magic crystal —" Simon took a deep breath, exhaling with a weariness of the weight of a whole dimension on his shoulders — "it is the key to finding Dracula's rib in Berkeley Mansion!"

"And I don't suppose you mean the barbecued type, do you?"

Simon looked at Tim with total confusion.

"Never mind. Dumb joke."

"You should try to be more serious, Timothy."

"Hey . . . it was my dumb jokes that drove Dracula off, wasn't it?"

"True. But you lack a certain gravity in your character."

"Well, I don't feel like I'm about to float off, if that's what you mean."

"This shall be one of my missions on this quest," said Simon. "I shall make you a more serious young man."

"And I," said Tim. "Will make you have a good laugh or two!"

Simon grunted. "We'll see." He turned and started marching off back to the exit of the church.

Tim tried his thorn whip. All he managed to do was to knock over a bunch of candles into a baptismal font. Their flames hissed out.

"Oh," said the voice of the brother, echoing with sarcasm through the church. "Wonderful. Thank you so much."

Tim wound the whip back up, grabbed his satchel and raced after Simon.

CHAPTER TEN

A Rib Tickler

Tim Bradley had seen some big, fancy houses in his life. But never before had he seen anything like Berkeley Mansion.

"Wow! Looks pretty intense!" he told Simon Belmont.

"An interesting word for a house of evil," said Simon grimly. Simon looked ill, as though he were struggling with something inside of him that he didn't want to talk about. "Berkeley Mansion was a bad place before Dracula ever came to Castlevania. It is a house where a great baron once killed his entire family, his servants and guests — and was there beheaded for his crimes by the law. They say that it is haunted by at least a thousand ghosts!"

Tim Bradley gulped. He could believe it. This house certainly looked like a haunted house, from the gothic architecture to the creepy mist that overhung it like a grave shroud. Even from outside, he could smell rotting timbers and the mustiness of hundreds of years of misuse.

This was one creepy place!

"Prepare, Timothy Bradley, for experiences that shall stretch and perhaps distort your mind!" A smile touched Simon Belmont's lips. "As we enter the doors of this great house, I am reminded of the beginning of one of your jokes, Timothy Bradley. 'Knock-knock!' "

Tim looked at Simon, and then back at Berkeley Mansion. "You want me to say 'Who's there?' Well, I'm not going to!" He took in a long breath. " 'Cause I don't really want to know!"

Tim Bradley had always wondered what a video game would look like if it became real. He'd always wondered about how the strange zigs and zags of a game would translate into three dimensions, along with taste and smell. However, he truly had never wanted to know what Castlevania would look like — it was too scary to contemplate!

However, now he knew.

And the truth was not pleasant.

This whole dimension seemed somehow tilted like an old horror movie. This was certainly the case with the interior of Berkeley Mansion. The floors and the ceilings and the walls just weren't square, just did not meet at right angles. The place not only smelled bad, it smelled very bad. It smelled of old shoes and dead socks. It smelled of forgotten things in the back of the refrigerator. It smelled of a terrible past unearthed — something better off buried.

The door was no problem. There was no door.

They walked into the main hallway

through the sagging open doorway. Draperies and tapestries hung in ruins all about a great hall to the the right. Clutter and antiques lay strewn in the wreckage.

"Which way?" Simon wondered, stroking his chin.

"I would think down, wouldn't you?" suggested Tim.

"Why would you say that?"

"I don't know — Dracula always likes to be close to the earth. Reminds me of the joke, why does a vampire take cold medicine?"

Simon made a face.

"To stop coffin!"

"I do not understand the joke, but your reasoning is correct. What else do you see here in this room that you think gives us information or might be of use?"

Tim surveyed the cluttered chamber. "Good thought. You know, the thing about Nintendo games is that there's always something around somewhere that you need to use somewhere else!"

"This is not a game of any kind," said Simon sternly. "This is deadly serious!"

"Yes, yes, I know . . . but I still think we should look for something that doesn't seem to belong here — something that looks like it might be useful later." Tim began to walk among the odds and ends. "Now look at this, for instance." He picked up a broken cuckoo clock. A bird on a broken spring hung out of it like a weird, alien tongue. "I don't see a thing that this would be good for." He tossed the thing back into a heap of junk. "But this . . . I don't know, it may be a possibility."

He bent down and pointed at something on the ground.

"What is it?" asked Simon.

It was an arrow. But not just any arrow — it looked like an Indian arrow, with colorful feathers on one end and a stone arrowhead on the other.

"Look at where it's pointed!" said Tim.

"At the fireplace. So?"

"I guess you wouldn't know, but these kind of mansions always have hidden passages. And they usually have them behind the fireplaces with marble mantlepieces."

Simon looked puzzled. "Why is that?"

"Because of these." Tim walked toward the fireplace. On the top of the mantlepiece was a row of candlesticks. "For hidden passages, you need handle openers." He pulled on one of the candles. It was just a candlestick and it came off.

"Ha! So much for your theories!"

"Please, Simon," said Tim still feeling self-confident on the subject. There were ten brass candlesticks on the mantlepiece, any one of which might be the secret handle that opened a hidden door.

Tim tried another candlestick. No go. Another. Nope. He started to get worried.

"Gee, I don't know. Maybe I am wrong. Maybe . . ."

Sticking out from the fireplace was an old grate. Looking over to Simon, he did not see it.

He tripped over it, falling flat onto his face.

"Oooph!" he said. His dignity was hurt far worse than his body.

"Tim, are you all right?" Simon rushed over to check, suddenly all seriousness again.

"Yeah. Stupid of me, but I'm kind of a klutz at home anyway. I — wait. What's that sound?"

The sound was a metallic scraping, like cement skidding along a steel floor.

Tim looked around at the same time that Simon did.

One of the dusty, cobwebby panels inside the fireplace was slowly sliding away, opening a section of musty, mysterious darkness.

Simon looked down at his fallen friend. "It would appear that I have an apology to make, Timothy Bradley!"

"Wow! There is a secret corridor!" Fear tickled his backbone. "On the other hand, how do we know for sure that this isn't a trap?"

Simon shook his head. "A trap would be more alluring, more obvious. No, you have done well. Let us progress. We, after all, have the torches we got at the inn to light our way."

"Yeah, lets just try not to burn down anything. This looks like a real firetrap here!"

Simon started for the passageway, his torch held out before him.

A sudden gust of wind blew out from the passageway, blowing out both torches.

The room was plunged into darkness.

"Well, so much for that!" said Tim. "Wait a minute though! That arrow! You know, maybe there's something magical about that arrow. I mean, it did show us the way to the passage."

"What do you mean?"

"Just a hunch. I mean, this sounds just like something from a video game. You need to find objects, you need to use objects. And sometimes those objects work together. So it follows that the arrow may affect whatever magic we've already gotten."

"The crystal! The crystal we got at the church!"

"It's worth a try, right!"

Tim heard the sound of uncertain footsteps as Simon searched his way back to the arrow. With a grunt, he knocked into something. Tim could hear the sounds of his hands feeling about the floor.

"Found it!" he said.

"Okay. Take the crystal and touch the arrowhead to it."

"Very well."

It was like turning on an electric light

bulb. The crystal ignited with a white light that lit the whole section of the room. Simon gasped with surprise and wonder, blinking with the brightness.

"I think that'll do the trick!" said Tim, brushing himself off as he got up. "Still, since you've got the light, maybe you should go first."

"Yes," said Simon. "Bring the torches, though. We could find a light later, and who knows how fickle this magical light will be!"

The passageway proved as dusty and murky as Tim had expected, but otherwise it was bare of danger. They followed it to a set of stairs which they descended. Three flights down, they came to a dead end. Simon, using the light, scoured the walls for some sort of opening.

He found nothing.

"Well, this is a fine fix!" said Tim, shaking his head. "I don't know, though. It doesn't really make sense, though, does it! I mean, why would there be a stairway down to a dead end?"

"You are the puzzle solver, Timothy."

"You know, you can call me Tim."

"Tim. Somehow it doesn't sound right." He stepped very close to the wall to inspect it closely, holding the arrow and the crystal up for better illumination.

And a very strange thing happened.

The crystal dulled in its brilliance.

The closer the magic thing got to the

wall, the lower dipped the light.

Simon stared at this phenomenon for a moment, drawing the crystal back and forth in the air to determine if in fact it was the wall that was dimming the crystal.

"Something evil is blocking this passageway!" he said. "Which means that it may be something that is protecting the rib of Dracula!"

"It looks that way. But how are we going to unblock it? We're not magicians. Should I start telling the wall jokes? Hey, wall! What's the stuff between an elephant's toes?"

"No, no. This time I know what to do!" Simon dug into his pack and drew out the large flask filled with the Holy Water they had received from the monk. "If indeed this is evil, it's not going to like this!"

He tossed a splash of the water upon the wall. The effect was immediate. It was as if Simon had tossed a stick of dynamite.

With a profound *kablam!* the whole wall caved in with a cloud of dust.

Tim took in a lungful and began coughing himself hoarse. However, he was gratified to see that the crystal was fairly bursting now with brilliance.

"You—" cough cough "—were right, Simon. Which reminds me of the joke about —"

Simon held up a hand. *"Shh!* Look into the next room, Tim!" He held forth the white crystal, which cast forth its light deep into the adjacent chamber.

Tim looked, and astonishment overtook him.

"My goodness!"

"Well don't just stand there," came a cackling voice like something out a rest home for witches. "Enter! If you dare!"

GAME HINT

To get to the last two mansions, bring the Red Crystal to Deborah Cliff and ride the tornado.

CHAPTER ELEVEN

Miss Ezederada

The next chamber was not the stark cellar room that Tim Bradley had expected.

Far from it.

Instead, it looked as though they had just knocked down the wall of Ye Olde Curiosity Shoppe.

At the very least, it seemed to be some sort of room filled with antique chairs, lamps, mirrors, knick-knacks, doo-dads, and whatnots, to say nothing of whatsits!

In the very middle of the room, sitting in a creaky old rocker was a creaky old lady with a very large black cat square in the middle of her ample lap, purring as it was petted.

"Come in, come in, you two! I'm not going to bite! I promise!" she said, with a reassuring matronly smile. "I can't thank you enough for knocking down that stupid, silly wall! I was just thinking about trying to start chipping away at with one of these sweet little antique sledgehammers over there, and that wouldn't have been very ladylike, now would it?"

Even though she was old and wrinkled, she was somehow very pretty, with a wealth of blonde curls above her head and a set of healthy white teeth behind a brilliant smile. Her eyes were bright blue. She fairly glowed with kindness, only dimmed by the paleness of being inside for so long. Tim liked her immediately. He had the feeling that not only was she of no harm to them, she might even be of help!

Simon evidently had the same impression. Tim could sense him relaxing his guard. "However do you find yourself down here, madam?" he asked politely. If Simon had been wearing a hat, Tim suspected that the valiant hero would have taken it off.

The old woman's eyes fairly glittered with good humor. "Well, now, there's an interesting story for you! But first things first! My name is Ezederada Perkins. And pray tell, who are these old eyes gazing upon?"

Tim and Simon introduced themselves.

"Simon Belmont! Well, hush my puppies! You wouldn't remember this, but I dandled you on my knee when you were just knee-high to a bat." Ezederada put her hand up to her mouth. "Oh, dear. How unfortunate a term. Especially in these circumstances!"

"Go ahead with your story!" urged Tim.

"Oh, dear, of course. How I do go on sometimes." She giggled almost girlishly. "You must understand, that I am the caretaker of Berkeley Mansion."

"Caretaker!" said Tim, unable to hide his surprise. Immediately he was embarrassed about his blurting out, but by the look of amusement in Ezederada Perkins's eyes, he could see that she didn't take it as an insult.

"Not what you think, Tim! You see, I take care that Berkeley Mansion looks ramshackle! I distribute the cobwebs, the dust, and the clutter just so. A work of art, I say, and it took years to get it this way! And now, that rascal Dracula has me locked down here, unable to appreciate my own handiwork!"

"However, thanks to you all, I am now free again! I can go up and drift through my lovely rooms and enjoy the delightful dilapidation!"

"That's all very well and good, Ezederada Perkins," said Simon. "However, we must tell you that we are on a very important quest!"

"Oh, yes, of course! You must be after the rib of Dracula. Well, it's downstairs, and you're welcome to it as far as I'm concerned. It's caused me absolutely nothing but a headache. The way it pounds on its drum sometimes!"

"Pounds on a drum?" said Tim.

"Yes, well, it hasn't got much else it can do, being just a rib and all. And I must say, it must feel a bit isolated without the rest of Dracula to keep it company. So it's got this silly drum and sometimes it pounds on it. What do you think? You think maybe it reminds it of the beat of its owner's heart?"

"I wouldn't think that Dracula had a heart!" said Tim.

"Oh, yes, and that is one of the things we must find," said Simon. "A heart, yes, but definitely a very black heart!"

"Yes, well, I daresay," said Ezederada. "None of my business. But anything I can do against Count Dracula will do my heart good!"

"How can you help us then?" asked Simon.

"Hmmmm. Let me see," Ezederada stroked her double chin. "Well, for starters, I can tell you how to get down safely to where the rib is located. And I suppose I might give you what you need to take the rib safely. Tricky business at best, that, and mind you, Count Dracula's minions may be stupid, but the count himself isn't. He's set up some safeguards for his rib!"

"We are prepared."

"Sorry, cat, but you're going to have to get off," said Ezederada, gently lifting the fat cat from her lap and placing it down on the floor. "Now then, let's see what we've got here!"

She turned her attention to a pile of junk in the middle of the room, pulling this out, pushing that aside.

"Sewing scissors. No. Thread. Won't help. Curling iron. Maybe with Dracula's hair, but not with his rib!"

She pulled out an old boot, a hat, a bicycle pump. "You find some strange things in haunted houses," she explained. "Even ghosts sometimes. Ah! What do you know!

Here's something I think you'll be able to use — a stake!"

Tim blinked. "What, to eat after we cook it on the barbecue with the rib?"

"No, no. You clearly think in puns, young man. An unhealthy habit. No." She held up a length of wood.

A stake! Oh, thought Tim. That kind of stake! It was long and had one blunt end and one pointed end.

"This is the kind of stake you'll need to deal with Dracula!" said the old woman.

She thrust it into Simon's hands. "Go down the staircase past that door. Take a left at the bottom and watch out for the troll.

"You'll see the dungeon to your left. There are skeletons hanging from chains. That's how you'll know you're in the right dungeon. Get past whatever monsters lurk down there, climb the steps, touch the rib with the stake — and hey, it's all yours. Bring it up here, dearies, so I can have a look at it, all right?" She started going through the junk on the floor again, humming a tune to herself, suddenly totally oblivious to the presence of the two heroes in her room.

"You'll give us more directions when we get back?"

"Hmmmmmm?" She turned around, smiling happily upon them. "Well, of course I will, loves! And also, there might be another goody or two that I unearth from this pile with your names on it. Toddle off now, then! Have a good time. Mind the monsters! Oh, and if you see the spirit of Dracula pop up, give the old blaggard my worst, will you?"

With that, Ezederada Perkins turned her attention back to her work.

"Off then!" said Simon Belmont, pointing with the stake toward the door. "To the dungeon!"

"To the dungeon with a bludgeon!" said Tim Bradley.

And off they went.

If the previous part of Berkeley Mansion had been dirty, then the dungeons below could be called absolutely, undeniably and irrefutably, totally filthy.

In short, a real mess.

"Maybe we should fire up the torches again, huh?" said Tim, chilled to the bone with the cold gloom into which they were descending.

"No. We shall make do with the white crystal. Look! See how nicely it glows, so close to the stake! This oaken stake must have magical properties as well. Good magical properties!"

"Well, all I can say is that I wish the good Lady Litter had given us a magical heater!"

"You are beginning to complain too much, Timothy Bradley! Did you think that a quest of this nature would be comfortable?"

Tim thought about that. True. When he sat down for a game of Castlevania, it was usually in his temperature-controlled room at home, be it air-conditioned or heated.

"All I can say is this experience certainly makes me appreciate heroes more!" He rubbed his rumbling stomach. "Especially hero sandwiches. Boy, could I use one right now, with some ham and cheese, salami and lettuce, tomato ... and gee, don't forget the hot peppers! Hold the mayo!"

"You are a very strange young man!" said Simon.

Tim laughed. He thought about digging into his pack for another hunk of chocolate, but he'd eaten so many already that he had to admit that even in this frightening and suspenseful moment, he was so chock full of chocolate that he just couldn't possibly indulge himself in another.

It was on the lower level, just where the lady caretaker had told them to expect it, that Tim and Simon encountered the troll.

It was not quite what they had expected.

CHAPTER TWELVE

Stake Out

That it was a monster there could be no doubt.

That it was the most peculiar monster that Tim Bradley had ever seen, in all the movies, comics, or television he'd experienced, there could be no doubt either.

"Good grief," Tim gasped, getting his sword ready.

"Prepare for battle, my fine assistant," shouted Simon Belmont, brandishing his whip. "I think we shall have an excellent little tussle against this one!"

The monster was tall. It walked like a man, but that was where the resemblance ended. It's face was like lizard hide. It's head looked as though someone had jammed a basketball through its fanged mouth. It looked, thought Tim, like the Creature from the Black Lagoon after a long spell on the wrong side of the lead shield in a nuclear reactor!

"*Arrrgh!*" it growled.

"Back, oh villainous creature of the night!" said Simon Belmont, bringing his arm back for a snap of the whip.

"Hey, hold on there!" said the thing. "I

said *argh* because I just stubbed my toe trying to get away from you guys. You wanna give me a break?"

"I do not trust you!" said Simon, and he flung the whip over his shoulder, perparing to strike.

However, Tim stepped in and stayed Simon's hand, causing the whip to strike the wall instead of the monster.

"Why did you do that!" screamed Simon Belmont, his face growing red.

"I don't remember if anger is one of those seven deadly sins," said Tim. "But you sure are getting out of control. I don't care how ugly the thing is — it's asked for a chance to explain what it's up to."

"But it is a creature of Dracula!" said Simon, growing more furious.

"Hey, simmer down, Simon. It looks like you're more a creature of Dracula now than it is! I mean, show a little mercy. Just because it's big, wicked-looking, and ugly doesn't mean it works for Dracula."

"Please!" said the creature. "Your companion is correct. Allow me to introduce myself. My name is Freddie."

"Say, no kidding. We have a guy in the horror movies back home. His name is Freddy, too."

"Ah, but 'Freddie' with an *i-e*?"

"Hmm. No, I suppose it's with a *y.*"

"Well, there you go! All good monsters have there names end with an *i-e*; all bad ones with a *y.* Helps keep things straight."

"Good monsters?" said Simon skeptically.

"Give a fella a break!" said Freddie, rearing to his full height with no small amount of indignity. A clatter of loose scales tumbled to the floor like snow. "I have a few bad habits, and we all lose our temper sometimes. But all in all, I must say, I'm a pretty nice guy."

"Why, then, has Dracula not possessed you?"

"Don't you think he hasn't tried? But you see, we smart monsters—" Freddie tapped his bulbous head cagily "—we know how to outwit the old skunk. It's the dumb ones that are in its sway. Not that we don't get tempted sometimes."

"Yes," said Simon. "I, too, have a temptation problem. This is one of the reasons that Timothy Bradley is here with me—to remind me that I am being tempted. And again, he has done an excellent job. And I thank him."

"And I thank him, too!" said Freddie, bloodshot thyroid eyes bulging almost comically. "But for you, good Sir Timothy, I most surely would have been snapped back into Ye Olde Nasty Dimension from whence all monsters, good and bad, arise. And let me tell you, that is not a nice place. No, I far prefer the twisted passages of Berkley Mansion and Veros Woods to that other dimension!"

"But that is where we're trying to send

Dracula, isn't it?" said Tim excitedly.

"Precisely!" said Simon. "But he stubbornly clings to this world. Why is this, Freddie Monster? What is the allure of the land of Castlevania, that Count Dracula should want to stay here when it would be so much easier for him to just let go and drift back to his home dimension?"

"Simple," said Freddie. "Here, he's big stuff. Back home, he's just another creep. Here, he's boss. Back there, he takes orders."

"But who from?"

"The biggest monster of them all, that's who. The Master of Death. Thanatos." Freddie Monster shivered. *"Gazookas!* It gives me the willies just to think about him! Just pray you don't ever run into him!"

"Thank you for your advice, Freddie Monster," said Simon with the utmost seriousness. "But perhaps you can be of further help to us."

"Sure! Advice I can give. But I can't help you to get Dracula. We've got sort of a truce, you see."

"That's all right," Tim said. "All we need is some help. The lady caretaker upstairs mentioned that there are all kinds of unpleasant creatures down in this cellar!"

"Oh, yes! She would! Well, we're just monsters, don't you know? Well, I guess I can put the word out. Can't guarantee much, though." Freddie smiled.

"Maybe you can also tell us where the dungeon with Dracula's rib is."

"Oh, sure, that smelly old thing!" Freddie Monster pointed a claw. "It's that way. Take a right at the fork."

"Thanks, Freddie," said Tim. "You've been a real help. You're a real credit to monsterdom!"

Freddie Monster took a deep bow, dislodging a number of small furry insects from the crevices on his body, all of which scurried back to his hairy feet for shelter. "Glad to be of service to you, gentlemen."

Tim and Simon bowed in return.

Then they headed deeper into the darkness of the dundgeons.

The skeletons were what tipped Tim to the fact that they were in the right place.

It was dark and dank, just like a dungeon was supposed to be. Somewhere water dripped. And in the distance monsters shuffled.

But it was when Tim smacked into the hanging bones that he knew they'd made it.

They hung from the ceiling like grisly decorations, grim reminders of exactly what sort of fellow this Dracula was. When Tim hit the bones, they clattered and clinked around like castenets on celebration day. Tim jumped back, scared nearly witless.

"*Yow!* Looks like bone day in biology class!" he said, trying to make a joke so he wouldn't be so spooked.

Simon grunted. "And look — on that platform up there! The item that we seek!"

Tim, still wary of these skeletons (in this world, you knew knew when skeletons would come alive and clatter down to grab ahold of your neck and squeeze!), stared up. "No bones about it — I mean, yeah, there it is!"

And there it was indeed.

The rib was bleached a bright white. It sat on a short pedestal and was encased in a globe made of crystal.

Simon strode toward the winding steps that led toward the rib.

However, before he could get very far, there was a sudden rumbling sound from deep in the earth. The floor shook. A fissure opened in the rock, and something emerged that made Tim want to just forget this whole thing, go run back to his home dimension and hide under his bed.

It was an eyeball.

A flying eyeball!

GAME HINT

When you get to Aljiba, buy garlic and laurels (you'll have to go through the floor to buy garlic).

CHAPTER THIRTEEN

The Ghostly Eyeball

"I see you!" said the eyeball.

It was a big thing, with trailing veins and surrounded by a ghostly mist of ectoplasm. It was mostly white, with blue and red pulsing blood vessels.

Unlike other eyeballs, however, this one had a big mouth filled with nasty, sharp teeth — as well as two arms filled with claws!

"*Yikes!*" said Tim. "You're just like Arnold Schwarzenegger's weight trainer!"

That stopped the Ghostly Eyeball in its tracks. "Whyever do you say that?"

"Because!" said Tim. "You've got a big pupil!"

The Ghostly Eyeball had no lids, so it could not blink.

It could only stare.

"Is that supposed to be funny?" it growled, gnashing its teeth sharply. "Stand back! You shall get no further! I am the guard for the rib of Dracula!"

"Wait! Didn't you talk to your buddy Freddie Monster?" said Tim.

"Freddie! Bah! He is no friend of mine!

And if he has turned on the master, then surely he is a traitor of the most heinous sort."

"I thought all you monsters were heinous!"

"*Bah!* Enough of this talk. Go away, or I shall devour you!"

"Sorry!" said Simon Belmont. "Our course is set! We must follow through! It is you who must stand aside."

The thing started for them.

Simon snapped his whip, striking the thing square in its cornea. The monster was only moved back mere inches, and then it advanced again.

Tim looked down at his own whip. He still hadn't gotten the hang of using it.

He dropped it and drew his sword. "How about a poke in the eye, Ghostly!" he said, swinging with all his might.

The Ghostly Eyeball flew nimbly aside, and Tim's swing went astray. He spun wildly. The blade whacked into one of the skeletons, knocking it apart. Bones flew everywhere.

"You see, you cannot harm me!" said the monster. "I see all! I"—"

Suddenly, the thing was enveloped by a cloth.

Simon Belmont had taken off his cloak and draped it nimbly over the creature. The thing tried to tear free, but it could not.

"I can't see!" It cried. "I can't see!"

Simon then took the arrow and jabbed it hard, under the edges of the cloth.

There was a loud *pop!*

A spume of green gases, smelling of bilge water, billowed out raggedly, followed by a burst of light; then the cape fluttered to the ground, limp as a flat tire.

"It's ... it's gone!" gasped Tim.

"Yes! Tossed back to its home dimension."

"The dimension of monsters!" Tim shivered. "That's one place I sure don't want to take a walk in on a cold and lonely night. Boy, Castlevania's bad enough."

But Simon wasn't listening. He was busy looking up at the pedestal, upon which rested the rib of Dracula.

With the Ghostly Eyeball gone, Tim felt much more self-confident about this whole business. "I'll get it!" he said, and rushed ahead of Simon.

Running smack into an invisible wall.

"Ouch!" he said, almost falling backward onto the floor. "I almost broke my nose."

"You know, I think that this arrow may help us again," said Simon. He advanced to the spot where the invisible wall had stopped Tim. He stabbed at the wall with the arrow's head. The wall shimmered like torn sandwich wrap.

Simon walked forward through where the wall had been, then up the steps. He touched the crystal globe with the arrow, and it, too, dissolved. Then he touched the rib of Dracula with the arrow.

The rib shuddered and radiated a faint sparkle.

He picked it up.

"We've got it!" said Simon triumpantly. "We've got the first part, Tim."

That was when the skeletons began to move. The skeletons shuddered and shook.

"*Yikes!*" said Tim. "Dracula's making no bones about the fact he doesn't like us." He stepped up to stand beside the blond hero, to be of help — and also enjoy the protection of Simon's excellent whip work.

When he turned, he saw the skeletons were joining together. And from their joined bones and skulls, a face was forming.

The face of Count Dracula.

"*Bah!*" he cried in a voice that sounded like the rattle-snap of thousand of bones breaking. "You think you have beaten me! But you have so much further to go yet. I have more tricks up my sleeve that will not be so easy for you to deal with. You shall not uproot me from my adopted home!"

Simon stepped forward. "I have sworn upon all that is good, true, and just, that you shall be removed from my beloved land of Castlevania — banished forever, never to return!"

"Right!" cried Tim, feeling full of himself. "You can go to New York City and visit the Vampire State Building!"

"Arggh!"

"Yes!" said Simon. "Go join the other pains-in-the-neck!"

"Pah!" The bones rattled with profound annoyance.

"Simon," said Tim, flabbergasted. "You made a joke! You actually told a joke!"

Simon seemed equally astounded. "My goodness! I did tell a joke!"

The vampire however was not amused. The skeleton bones he had possessed shook and rattled. Bones and teeth began to flake off and clatter to the dungeon floor.

"You shall not beat me, mortal!" cried the voice of Dracula as it echoed away. "You shall not best my powers, I swear!"

And then, with the howling of a terrible wind, the spirit essence ripped away from the dungeon.

The skeleton bones all tumbled to the floor in a huge heap.

"We did it!" cried Tim. "We beat Dracula."

However, Simon Belmont was not convinced. "We have far to go yet, Timothy Bradley. Very far to go!"

CHAPTER FOURTEEN

You Take the High Road, I'll Take the Low Road, and I'll Get into Trouble Before You!

Several hours later, in the middle of the Aljiba Woods, Tim Bradley's satchel — the one with all his chocolate — flew away and splashed into the center of a quicksand pool.

It sank without a trace.

Tim, who had just fallen flat on his face after tripping over a root in the path, watched all this with a horror approaching panic.

His chocolate! His lovely chocolate! All his Hershey bars were in that sack. And his M&M's! The M&M's with peanuts, too, just the one's he'd been craving! All his chocolate was gone.

Something wrenched inside of him. He felt like screaming, but he couldn't let it out. Simon would hear him. Simon had taken Tim aside and told him that maybe he was eating far too many chocolate bars to be good either for his nerves or for his health. Tim had asked him if Simon thought he were his mother, for goodness' sake, and Simon had said no, but as leader on this quest he felt that he should point these things out.

Deep down, Tim Bradley knew that Simon was right. Simon had pretty quickly figured out that Tim was hooked on this stuff, and that it wasn't particularly good for him. So Tim had agreed he wouldn't have another candy bar for two hours.

So, of course, one hour later, he had desperately craved one, and he'd snuck off behind some trees and —

Well, he'd lost all his chocolate!

And things had been going so well, too!

Miss Perkins, the lady custodian of Berkeley Mansion, had told them that she'd had a vision. Their next destination would be Rover Mansion. But how pray tell, they asked her, would they get to Rover Mansion since they had no map.

"Go to the town of Veros," the woman had said. *"One of the gentlemen in the resistance movement will sell you a special dagger."* Also, there was a chain whip available. This chain whip would come in very handy, Miss Perkins had promised them.

Simon had no idea what a chain whip was, but when they went to Veros and found the man and bought it, he was quite pleased. The "chain" was actually a specially pleated material — very strong, with almost a magical feel to it. The dagger was very nice as well, a shiny silver thing. They checked the signpost to see where they should go next.

The signpost had directed them to Aljiba Woods.

There they had discovered a wall that shone most magically.

"I have to check this!" Simon had said, which was okay by Tim, since he felt like resting anyway. Simon found it impossible to cross the wall on his own, so he'd tried splashing it with Holy Water, the tactic that had been so helpful back in Berkeley Mansion. It worked. The wall had fallen down. Beyond it had been a glowing fire in a dish. "A Sacred Flame!" Simon had cried. "Something I'd hoped we'd come across." Simon re-lit their torches from the Sacred Flame, and told Tim that he felt much less tempted under its light.

Which was okay with Tim, since he was tired of keeping track of the hero's odd mood swings.

And so here they were — Aljiba Woods — and everything was absolutely hunky-dory.

Except for the fact that Tim had just lost his chocolate.

"Timothy!" cried Simon Belmont from the trail that the signpost had called Dabi's Path. "Timothy Bradley! Where are you?"

"Over here!" cried Tim, picking himself up and dusting himself off. He hurried back onto the path.

Simon was anxious to keep moving. "We've still got a lot of Dracula's body parts to find," he said. "And very little time in which to do it."

Together they set off again through the night.

Imagine! thought Tim. Me, the chocolate

freak, in a land without chocolate.

Oh, well, he'd just have to live without it.

If you could call it living.

The town of Aljiba looked much like the other towns they'd visited in Castlevania except that maybe it was darker, maybe it was dirtier, maybe it felt like the spirit of Dracula was even more in control.

All in all, it made Tim happy that this flame that was lighting their path was sacred. For Aljiba felt absolutely evil.

"Just over here, I think!" called Simon. He stepped quickly down the cobblestones, holding up his torch. The illumination showed a sign depicting a vampire with long fangs, pointed ears, a bat on his shoulder — and an red NO sign stamped over him.

"The Ye Olde Anti-Vampire Shoppe," Simon explained. "Come in with me, Tim. We'll get some things we need here."

"Uhmm — don't you think that this is one place that Dracula will be sure we'll go? I mean, he'll have a trap or something set up, right?"

"No. He despises the things that are kept inside — and besides, the owner will be the one person in Aljiba who will be openly defiant of Dracula's rule! Come, hurry, Timothy! There is absolutely no time to waste."

Simon went through the door. A bell tinkled. Thinking it a trap, Tim jumped. He was ready to run, but then he realized, Hey, a tinkling bell when you go into a shop is perfectly normal. Cool it, pal.

He went through the door.

He found himself in a shop that smelled of a curious blend of tobacco, vinegar, spices of various sorts, and, most strongly, of garlic. On the wall were displayed crosses of various shapes and sizes, some wooden, some silver, some made of other stuff. The place looked like an Italian deli, what with all the strings of garlic bulbs stretched around the room. Other stuff hung hither and thither, none of which Tim recognized. Whatever they were, it followed that they must have something to do with getting rid of vampires.

The shop was warm and cozy, and Simon had been right — Tim felt safe here. This was like an oasis of safety in a desert of danger!

"Yes. May I help you?" asked a suspicious voice.

"Edward! My good friend!" said Simon. "Do you not recognize me?"

"Simon? Simon Belmont?" A big man dressed in a frayed topcoat stepped from the darkness of the back room. He wore a plaid scarf around his neck even though the room was toasty warm, and he looked at them from above half-frame reading spectacles. He held out a large, hairy hand — but then, suddenly, he pulled it back. "Wait a moment! Are you not aligned now with that demon Dracula?"

"I am the person who vanquished him!"

"I have heard that you struggle yet with his infection!" growled the man in a bearlike, gruff voice. "There is no way of telling whether or not you have succumbed to his domination. His presence floats now everywhere."

"Old friend! How would I be able to last fifteen seconds in the garlic soup of this atmosphere?"

The man's wide face split into a grin, showing yellowed teeth. "Your logic is irrefutable! I wish we had time for a game of chess, yes?"

"I'm afraid there are matters of far more gravity than chess, my friend," said Simon. "But allow me to introduce you to my new friend."

Simon introduced Tim, who was surprised to be swept up in a great big, garlicky bear hug. "Anyone who is a friend to the great hero of Castlevania, Simon Belmont, is a friend of mine!" said the burly man. "My name is Edward Farquar."

Simon quickly filled Edward in on their adventures. "We were told by Miss Perkins when we left Berkeley Mansion that we would most definitely need lots of garlic and lots of laurels. And I knew exactly where to get it all!"

"You came to the right place for garlic!" laughed Edward Farquar. "But as for laurels, I can't say! I'll have to dig deep into my supply room. May I ask, why laurels? They are a symbol of victory, and that seems a long way away, if I may say so?"

"The power of positive thinking!" piped Tim.

Both Castlevanians looked at him as though he were from another dimension.

Which was okay, Tim guessed, because he was.

"Well then," said Edward Farquar, becoming serious. "Perhaps I'd better go and see about those laurels." With no further adieu he turned around and walked into the darkness of the back room. A light flicked on, and Tim could hear the big man grunting as he rummaged through packages and stored materials galore.

"Gee," said Tim. "I hope he's got some laurels. Miss Perkins was very specific. 'You're going to need laurels,' she said. 'Most definitely laurels.' "

"I have every confidence in my friend," said Simon. "If there are laurels to be had anywhere in Castlevania, it is in this shop!"

Tim said, "Whatever you say. I just —"

Suddenly, a teddy bear sailed through the opening, bouncing against the opposite wall and landing face up, button eyes staring up at Tim. Immediately afterward, a stuffed giraffe followed its cloth cousin. Then, immediately afterward, a stuffed koala bear.

"What does he have back there?" said Tim. "A kiddie zoo? Which reminds me, Simon. Who is beautiful, gray, and wears a glass slipper?"

"Tim, I hardly think —"

"Cinderelephant!"

"I don't understand."

"C'mon, c'mon. You've heard the story of Cinderella and the glass slipper — I mean, you could have been Prince Charming yourself, Simon."

Simon blinked. "Prince Charming?"

"Never mind. You really are no fun, you know?"

"This is not a fun situation, Timothy. My very soul is at stake, to say nothing of the future of my beloved Castlevania."

Tim felt the definite craving for chocolate. Now! All this seriousness, and especially all this garlic were getting to him. However, his sinking feelings were interrupted by yet more objects hurtling from the back room.

"Gadzooks!" Simon cried to Edward Farquar. "Where did you get all this stuff?"

Farquar stuck his big head out. "In truth, I do not know. When I inherited this shop, much of what I own now was already here. I attempted to catalog it, but ..."

"But what does this have to do with vampires?" asked Simon impatiently.

"Absolutely nothing. But isn't it neat?"

"Edward," said Simon in a chastising manner. "We really do need those laurels."

"Oh, yes, of course. Right away. Laurels." The head ducked back into the back room. A minute more and it poked back outside. "I think I have what you're looking for here, Simon!" He brought out a handful of branches from a laurel tree. "Astonishingly fresh for sitting around these past few centuries, I must say. I never noticed them before. They were sitting on top of this mirror here. I must say, I hadn't noticed the mirror either." He pulled it out. It was a rolling mirror, a great oval golden thing.

And its glass was cloudy, just like the signpost back in Castlevania.

Cloudy, and getting cloudier. Great murky billowing puffs of gray were boiling across its surface.

And then Tim noticed that a face was becoming visible in the mirror.

"Simon," said Tim. "Look. I think we have company!"

GAME HINT

To get to the second mansion, you need the blue crystal.

CHAPTER FIFTEEN

Red Rover, Blue Rover, Will You Come Over?

In the mirror was the beautiful face of Linda Entwhistle.

It was enough to make Tim Bradley forget all about chocolate. She was so beautiful his heart leapt up and he could think of nothing else but pleasing her.

"Linda! Hello!"

"Hello, Tim," she said. "I cannot stay long. I came because there is great danger. There is . . . " She started fading in and out of focus. " . . . trouble in the . . . "

"Linda," said Simon, stepping forward. "We can't hear you! Speak up!"

Her image flickered in the mirror, like bad reception on a TV screen. "Cannot speak long," she managed to say. "Your energy is running low, and there are no ghouls now in Aljiba. You must find a man in a gray suit from the resistance movement. He will upgrade your white crystal into something more powerful. This will give you more energy."

What would really give him some energy, thought Tim, would be some serious chocolate!

"From there you must find your own way!" said Linda.

And then, as suddenly as she had come, she disappeared.

"Linda!" cried Simon.

"A most curious emanation!" said Edward Farquar, clearly quite surprised.

"A man in gray," said Tim. "What could she mean by that?"

Simon shook his head, baffled. "There must be a hundred men in gray. I know not!"

"Ah!" said Edward Farquar, his broad face beaming. "But perhaps I do!"

"You do? Well, do not hide it, my friend."

"There is a man across the square named Harrelson. He is a cobbler by trade, but he always wears gray. There is no other citizen of Aljiba for whom gray is constant apparel."

"That's it, then!" Simon said, tucking the garlic and laurels into his backpack. "Thank you, my good friend! Come, Tim! We must go find the Man in Gray!"

Sure enough, Simon Belmont found the Man in Gray just where Edward Farquar had promised he would be — in his cobbler shop. However, the man — Richard Harrelson by name — was hardly as cooperative as Simon's friend in the anti-vampire shop had been.

For one thing, he claimed he needed money for the crystal upgrade. "Can't give away these things free," he said. "A man's got to make a livin', ya know? And I reckon from the looks of you — I mean with those blond locks and those muscles I take you to be a hero and probably a wealthy man. So why should I let you take me for a fool, eh?"

Simon was aghast at this. "I am not a rich man by any means. I serve goodness and right!"

The man — a fellow with a weasly narrow face and greasy hair pasted across his forehead — gave a sneaky smile. "Ah, yes, but this nose —" he touched his ratlike snout "— this proboscis of mine smells coins, and these ears —" he tapped a hairy lobe "— they hear the jingle of coins, no?"

"In truth, I do have a few coins in my pocket. And perhaps I can spare one for your trouble in this matter. But only one, I think!"

Tim got exasperated. "Look, Simon, I'm going to leave you two to your bargaining. I'm just going to go around into the alley for a minute." Tim turned around and walked back into the street, leaving the duo to negotiate their deal.

Actually, he was sort of half-hoping that he'd run across some chocolate or at least something sweet. But of course there was no chocolate in Castlevania. No, strike that. There was chocolate in Castlevania — but now it was at the bottom of that quicksand!

What a place!

He knew that if he could just hang in there, he'd be triumphant along with Simon. Hadn't his experience with video games taught him that? If you got beat, you started over and kept trying. What was the word for it. *Perseverance*. That's right. He had to persevere.

Still, all the same he could sure do with a Hershey's Kiss!

"Hello!" came a voice from the darkness. Tim started.

"Who's there?" he demanded. He held out his torch, and a solitary figure stepped into the light.

It was a girl. A young girl about his age. She was cute, too, with dark eyes and dark hair and a smile that reminded Tim of Carol Jance back home. "Just me. My name is Melanie. You look like someone I can trust. I need someone that I can trust!"

"Oh...well, my name is Tim. Actually, I'm Simon Belmont's assistant. We're taking a tour of the country, picking up — er, picking up this and that. For the good of Castlevania, you understand."

Her eyes sparkled with good humor. "Oh. You mean you're going to kick Dracula out, so we can get some sunshine!"

"Yeah! I guess you could say that, Melanie!"

"Well, I'm all for that. I could use a little sunshine. You will be my friend, won't you?"

"Sure. Why not?"

"Here, would you like a piece of chocolate?"

Bells rang. Somewhere in Tim's mind, trumpets sounded. Chocolate? Did she say chocolate?

"Yeah!" he said, reaching out. But just as he was about to take hold of the candy that the girl was offering him, something stopped him.

What was a girl doing with this stuff?

"Wait a second," he said, not knowing whether or not to be suspicious, but pretty sure that something was rotten in Castlevania. "Simon Belmont says there is no chocolate in Castlevania!"

"I get it from a special place!" Melanie said. "Go ahead. Take it. It's a chocolate truffle. Godiva chocolate!"

Godiva's, of course, were some of the very best chocolates there were. And suddenly, Tim could almost smell the piece of chocolate. The scent of sweet ecstasy wandered under his nose.

He could almost taste it! He felt an almost uncontrollable urge to reach out and grab that candy and cram it into his mouth.

But he restrained himself.

"What's wrong?" asked Melanie. "Don't you trust me?"

"No, I don't trust you. This is just a trick ... Dracula."

Suddenly, Melanie's face began to distort and change. Her nose grew, and fangs came out of her mouth. After a few seconds, her true identity was revealed. Melanie was really Dracula in disguise!

Smiling, Dracula turned to Tim. "Stop interfering and head back to your own dimension. If you leave now, I'll give you all the chocolate you can eat!"

"No!" said Tim.

"What?" said the vampire.

"No!" said Tim, forcibly stopping himself. "No, I'm not going back until we've kicked your sorry spirit back to the dimension where it belongs!"

The result in the vampire was radical. At first the fearsome face showed nothing. Then disbelief flickered, to be replaced immediately by an explosion of hate and fury.

"Impossible! Nobody resists the temptations of Dracula! Has it occurred to you, you little piece of rot, that because of this decision you may never, ever taste the extraordinary tastebud pleasures of chocolate again?"

Tim cringed. That hadn't occurred to him, and he wasn't sure if Dracula was bluffing — but even if he was, the young man intended to stick to his guns.

"I don't care. Now just go away. You can't hurt me. You don't even have a body!"

"Little rodent! Very well! But I warn you, you shall regret this day for the rest of your life!"

And so saying, Dracula disappeared in an explosion of color and fizzling fireworks and a stink like moldering leftovers forgotten too long in the refrigerator.

Tim left in a hurry. It did not seem like a good idea to stay in this alley. No, not at all.

Heading out, he ran directly into Simon Belmont.

"My gracious, you're in a hurry! And you look like you've just seen your own ghost!"

Tim held his tongue on the Dracula business. No reason to alarm his traveling companion unduly. "This place is not the most comforting spot in the universe. Did you get the stuff?"

Simon held up the crystal. It was no longer white; it flashed with the bluest blue that Tim had ever seen, the color of blue where the ocean meets the sky. "It cost me more than I'd hoped it would, but I got what we need."

"Well then, what are we waiting for? Which way do we go?"

Simon smiled and looked down at the glowing blue with wonder. "Come, my friend. I have the feeling that the light is shining on us now, and perhaps the way from here on out will be smooth."

CHAPTER SIXTEEN

The Slime of Dracula

It was the ugliest, most frightening creature that Tim Bradley had ever seen and it was staring him right in the face.

"I'm going to eat you," the thing said, and Tim believed it. Its mouth dominated its body and was plenty large enough to swallow both Tim and Simon Belmont in one crunching gulp.

To make matters even worse, it had the worst case of halitosis that Tim had ever experienced. Its breath smelled like Tim's big brother's gym bag. It trembled before them now like a mound of mud and leaves, dripping and slobbering.

The duo were in Belasco Marsh. Things had gone well, just as Simon had predicted. They had discovered Dracula's heart in Rover Mansion, and added it to their collection, safely tucked away in Simon Belmont's bag. Then they'd added Dracula's brain. They'd also found directions to their next destination. Unfortunately, they had to go through Belasco Marsh to get there, and landed in this spot of trouble.

"I," said the creature, shivery and quaking like some mutant mound, "am Slimey BarSinister. And you are dead."

The thing had simply risen up out of a large pool of fetid water just seconds ago. From the look of it, it meant business.

Serious business.

"I'm afraid that I shall have to take issue with that proclamation!" said Simon. Taking a step back, he pulled out the chain whip and snapped it at the monster. The whip sliced through the thing called Slimey BarSinister with a loud snap.

An eyeball rolled out of the mass and plopped right in front of Tim, staring up with alarm.

"*Yeow!*" said Slimey BarSinister. "Why'd you do that?" With a grunt, it slipped out a tentacle, grabbed ahold of the eye and stuck it back into its face.

"We have every right to defend ourselves!" said Tim. "After all, we don't particularly want to be eaten!"

"You don't?"

"No, of course not! Don't be silly!" said Simon. "Now if you don't dive back to where you were, I intend to promptly send you back to your home dimension!"

"Hmmm." The thing rolled its eyes thoughtfully. "Count Dracula told me that you would quite enjoy being eaten. I was rather looking forward to it, myself, though I must admit that I've never eaten a human before."

This thing was truly huge, and Tim could see that whip and sword or no whip and sword, he and Simon where not far from a trip down this thing's gullet. "Oh, you wouldn't like it. Not at all!"

"No? Why not?"

"We taste like fish!"

"Yum. I do like fish."

"Dead fish?"

"The very best kind!"

Tim thought feverishly. "Actually we taste like — taste like ... chocolate!" Tim winked desperately at Simon. C'mon old boy! Understand this one!

Slimey BarSinister wrinkled the appendage that Tim presumed to be his nose. "Chocolate! What is that?"

"Believe me, Slimey!" said Simon, with a face of such seriousness that only a hero of Simon's magnitude could conjure it up. "You don't want to know what chocolate is!"

This statement and the clear sincerity with which it was spoken had a profound impact upon Slimey BarSinister. The creature — before a sickly green and chartreuse in color — abruptly turned shades of blue, red, and purple, his skin rippled like old pudding.

"Euchhhh!"

"You see, Slimy, you want absolutely nothing to do with eating us. Dracula lied to you. We're totally indigestible." Tim stepped forward, bravely holding out a hand. "Here you go. Have a lick if you want. Taste test!"

The creature quivered back like an

amoeba. "Nooooooooo. Get away, you foul disgusting creature!" it said. "Don't touch me! *Argggh!*"

"You had best watch out, thing!" said Simon, waving his whip threateningly. "Else he will tell you a silly joke, or worse make a bad pun!"

This was simply too much for Slimey BarSinister. "No! Please! Anything but that!"

"Why did the monster cross the road?" snapped Tim.

Slimey BarSinister slunk back, holding out his tentacles to ward off his attackers. "No, please!"

"You must tell us where the next piece of Dracula is!" commanded Simon.

"And while you're at it, why don't you tell us *what* the next piece of Dracula is!"

"Why, it's Dracula's eyeball, of course!" said Slimey BarSinister. "And it's in Brahm's Mansion of course. Just take the lower path yonder." He pointed over to a weed patch.

"What else can you tell us?" demanded Simon.

"You need not have feared me! I see you have laurels. Merely wear them beneath your undergarments and no other creature of these woods can harm you!"

"Sounds kinda itchy to me. But maybe it's worth it."

"Can I go now?"

"Yes, of course you can go!" said Tim. "Scoot! Skedaddle! Vamoose!"

The floppy creature took three wobbly

steps and then jumped back into the sludge.

"So much for that joker!" said Tim Bradley, brushing his hands symbolically.

"Yes, quite true," said Simon. "Yet why do I have the feeling that things might not go so well in the future?"

A shiver raced up Tim Bradley's spine.

He knew somehow that Simon Belmont was right.

GAME HINT

Go to Dabi's Path and break through the wall to get the sacred flame.

CHAPTER SEVENTEEN

Thanatos

Simon Belmont and Tim Bradley emerged from the fourth mansion, Simon holding his prize along with the other body parts in his canvas sack.

Dracula's eyeball.

"Well," said Tim, feeling pretty good. "Of the four parts we've found so far, I guess Dracula's brain doesn't add much weight to that sack!"

"His cunning must be in his entire body," said Simon. "You should not underestimate him, Tim."

It was then that Thanatos (the Master of Death, remember?) showed up.

Brahm's Mansion had been much the same as Rover Mansion, which had also been quite like the other grand decaying houses holding the body parts of Dracula. Right up to the skeletons in the dungeon! Oh, well, it also made things a little simpler. Not that they hadn't gotten their share of monsters and creepy-crawlers, to say nothing of shivers. However, for some reason Dracula had been leaving Simon pretty much alone. And now that Tim seemed to have kicked the chocolate habit, he felt much better about things, much better, in fact about this whole business. In fact, he was actually starting to think that this was going to be a very positive experience after all.

That was, until the Master of Death showed up.

Thanatos erupted out of thin air, right in front of the path to the forest like a bolt of lightning in the middle of a thunder storm. When Tim's eyes recovered from the blast of sizzling white light, he opened them and saw the thing standing in front of them.

"Heaven help us!" said Simon Belmont, flinging his whip back into readiness — as though that would help. From the size of this guy it looked as though it was going to take a lot more than just a whip, even if it was a magical chain whip to deal with him.

Tim Bradley could not speak, let alone come up with a cute quip.

This joker was absolutely incredible.

"I am Thanatos, Master of Death!" said the big guy. "Look on me and despair!"

He seemed to be about twenty feet tall, with legs like the trunks of trees, arms with biceps that would make Arnold Schwarzenegger gasp with envy and a chest as thick as a Sherman tank. But it was as much his outfit as his size that made Tim freak out almost totally.

Thanatos looked like a hood straight out of Flatbush, Brooklyn, in the 1950s, who had made a time stop in the current heavy-metal era for some jewelry.

He wore black leather pants with a

black shirt, littered with chains and spangles and other cheap jewelry. He wore the classic black leather motorcycle jacket. On his wrists were leather bracelets with studs.

His face was like a cross between something out a fifties' horror movie and someone out of a forties' gangster film. His entire face was broad. His hair was cut flattop style. There was a ring in his nose, making him look much like a bull who'd just stepped off a motorcycle after a high speed dust up with the cops.

"You, I shall toss back to your home dimension!" Thanatos said to Tim Bradley, gesturing with a hand the size of Tim's room. "And you, Simon Belmont—" he lifted his boots so high that Tim could see the hobnails on the bottom "—you I shall crush!"

Simon Belmont looked unfazed at this threat. Tim guessed that was one of the nice things about being a hero. You didn't get too upset when big guys threatened you. You just took it all in stride and figured that this was just the next part of your mission or quest or duty.

Tim, on the other hand, did not consider himself a hero. Tim considered himself a fourteen-year-old who had stumbled into something that he really didn't want to be in, but who had decided that it was best for all involved that he see the whole thing through to the end.

Now, however, he wasn't so sure. All the other parts of this journey had been scary and frightening sure, but they had been fun compared to this guy. This guy really and truly meant business. And when he killed someone, that person was dead with a capital *D*. And who knew, maybe worse than dead!

The thing started to advance, pounding forward like a Japanese horror movie made real. The spangles and jewelry flashed with an infernal light of their own. The smell of the thing advanced before it, a wave of seaweed and dead jellyfish. The very air began to crackle with energy.

Simon Belmont cracked his whip, but it snapped against some kind of force field. The tip exploded into a shower of sparks.

Fear grabbed Tim Bradley. He felt as though his courage were seeping through the bottoms of his feet. He had the almost uncontrollable urge to turn and run just as hard as he could.

Simon Belmont flicked the whip back again. His face was resolute, sure of victory. He hurled the whip . . .

And then the impossible happened.

Thanatos, Master of Death, reached out with one of his hands, and he reached out so quickly that Tim could barely see him move. The hand shot out, wrapped around Simon's body, and pulled him forward toward his face. The mouth opened, and Tim had a glimpse beyond jagged fangs and rotting molars . . . a glimpse of stars and nebulae, of shadows between planets and worlds being born and worlds dying.

The hand pulled Simon Belmont toward his death.

Almost unable to stop himself, Tim turned to run. He had to get out, had to get away! Had to, had to . . .

But then he stopped. He forcibly called himself to a stop, got a grip on that fear that had grabbed him with every bit as much force as the Master of Death had used to grab Simon.

No! He was bigger than his fear.

Besides, hadn't Thanatos said something . . .

Something very important, something very telling . . .

"Stop right there, this instant!" called Tim Bradley. "Don't you dare eat that hero!"

He said it with such authority and such loudness that Thanatos did stop. He held Simon Belmont dangling just inches from the chasm of nothingness and his eyes rolled like bloodshot marbles toward Tim Bradley, looking down as a cook might on some troublesome mouse *squeeking* for cheese in the pantry.

"Who dares challenge Thanatos, Master of Death?" the great leather being demanded.

"Look, you jerk, we know your name by now." Tim took out his whip. He didn't really know how to use it, but he sure could try and fake it.

"How dare you speak to me like that, mortal!"

"Look, I may be mortal, but I can thrash you any day, you third-rate creature feature."

The Master of Death began to turn a bright purple. Steam spumed from his ears. He dropped the half-conscious Simon Belmont to the ground and started stomping toward Tim, lightning bolts and firecrackers exploding from his bulging eyes. "You're worse than dead, buddy boy."

"Oh, no, I'm not!" Tim hurled the whip with all his might, snapping it just like Simon Belmont had taught him to. And lo and behold, the whip cracked.

And it cracked like the voice of doom.

Thanatos stopped in his tracks. He looked down at Tim much in the way a crocodile in combat boots might look at a snail it is about to step on who has just lifted up and displayed an atomic bomb it is about to detonate.

"Who *are* you?"

"Timothy Bradley!" said Tim. "And who, pray tell are *you?*"

"I am —" Thanatos shook his head, confused. "I have already told you who I am, Timothy Bradley. What do you use for a head, a pumpkin?"

Tim snapped the whip again. The sound was louder. It was as though something deep and wonderful inside him had taken control of his arm.

The creature actually stepped back, looking perplexed.

Meanwhile, off to the right, Thanatos

did not notice that Simon Belmont was recovering. Simon was slowly getting to his feet, looking around him dizzily.

Tim knew he had to distract the thing's attention. He had to let Simon get another chance at it!

"I've got a computer for a brain, you stupid pile of buttons!" cried Tim. "I'm a lot smarter than you!"

"You are an arrogant piece of ear wax, Timothy Bradley!" Angry smoke spumed from the thing's armpits. "I shall have to kill you now!"

"But you can't kill me! You said so yourself! You can only send me back to my home dimension!"

The monster was taken aback. His mouth hung open.

"I was being merciful, you brat! I can do what I like!"

"Oh, yeah?" Tim snapped his whip again. "Well come and get me, cucumber breath!"

The thing snarled like a million cats, fighting. It stepped forward.

Tim stepped forward to meet it and flung the whip again. "Death, here is thy sting!"

Snap!

And again!

Cr-rack!

The video game master's reflexes had been honed to perfection. He could actually do this now! He could use the whip! And here was the proof!

For he had just flicked the whip so expertly that it had caught Thanatos directly on the tip of his big nose!

"Yeeee — ouch!"

Where the whip tip had landed was a red welt that immediately spread through the nose. It swelled up hugely, almost obscuring the creature's bowling-ball eyes!

"Stand back, you foul thing!" said Tim, raging against the night, raging against the Master of Death, screaming at the top of his lungs. "And while you're doing that, why don't you just get back where you belong and never come back again!"

"What?" blustered Thanatos. "You wound me and then you order me about? You shall pay! You shall pay dearly, mortal!"

From the corner of his eye, Tim could see that Simon was getting up. He was reaching into his pocket for something. Tim had to keep the creature's attention diverted.

"So far, all I have gotten is more and more blasts of hot air, Thanatos! Come on. Show me what you can do, big boy!"

Quaking with fury, the monster charged Tim.

However, Simon Belmont leapt into action.

Literally.

He jumped upon the creature's back, flinging the whip around its neck.

Then he jammed one eye with the blue crystal, and the other with a batch of garlic cloves, blinding the monster.

Thanatos howled with vexation and fury.

"Strike him in the chest, Tim! Strike him in the chest!"

Tim ran up and hit Thanatos in the chest with a clenched fist.

"No!" said Simon, fighting for all he was worth to stay on the creature, who was bucking like a Brahman bull. "With the thorn whip. With the thorn whip, Tim!"

"Oh."

Tim stepped back, aimed and let go.

Snap!

The biggest *snap* off all!

Thanatos gave one more mighty heave, tossing Simon Belmont off once more.

However, he did not look as though he were about to charge Tim any longer.

In fact, the Master of Death looked like he was very ill, or about to explode.

Or perhaps both.

His edges turned to shimmering flames and he shook like a leaf. His clothing turned almost translucent and began to crack.

"I do believe that Thanatos needs a little more assistance to negotiate his way back where he belongs." Simon pulled his flask of Holy Water out and tossed it on the vibrating monster.

It was like tossing gasoline on flames.

Thanatos winked like an exploding star — and then, with a final snarl, he collapsed into nothingness as though sucked away by a black hole.

"Wow!" said Tim. "What a sight!"

Simon Belmont took a deep breath and put away first the flask and then the crystal.

Then he looked at Tim with renewed respect.

And perhaps even awe.

"Do you realize who that was?" he said.

"My gosh, do I have to say the name again. Thanatos, Master of Death!"

"Yes, but do you have any idea what that monster could have done to you!"

Tim made a motion of dismissal with his hand.

"Ah, no big thing. He was just as full o hot air as Dracula."

Simon shook his head solemnly. "You were really in big trouble, Tim! Your bravery is truly astounding!"

Tim blinked. "Uhm, you meant I really could have — er — died?"

Simon said, "In a word . . . yes!"

Tim Bradley fainted dead away.

CHAPTER EIGHTEEN

The Final Confrontation: Part One

Hours later, after Tim had recovered from his faint, after other adventures and other creatures, after a great deal of whip work (for he could now wield a whip in reality as well as he could on a game machine), after recovering the final part of Dracula (a foot, as it turned out), both Tim Bradley and Simon Belmont were very, very tired.

So it was no surprise at all to Tim Bradley when Simon Belmont sat down near a tree stump near the town of Alder and said, "I am so tired, Timothy Bradley. We must rest for a while."

Now Tim was fatigued as well. After all, you can't go through close to two days of monsters, vampires, and the Master of Death without feeling a certain amount of weariness. They were in the town of Alder now. It was dark and cold and all the colors of night pressed in on them as they sat in a small park, beneath some trees. There were no lights in any houses, nor were there any taverns to welcome them with warmth and song. All was dead quiet. Or was the right term *quietly dead?* Tim Bradley did not care to find out.

"I don't know, Simon. Maybe we'd better just press on and get this over with."

"No," said Simon. "I must rest. Give me just ten or fifteen minutes. Let me refresh myself. Then we can be on our way."

"Okay. But maybe I'd better just stay awake and keep watch."

"Yes, yes, that would be a good idea. You are a good companion, Timothy Bradley. You are a good friend. I could not have come so far without you! The way you dealt with the Master of Death. The way you leapt those mystical blocks! And especially without your help, we would not have been able to get that boat across the river and procure this magical diamond!" Simon held up the gem. It sparkled in the light of their torch.

"Well, we've got a ways to go, haven't we? Now you rest, Simon, if that's what you've got to do. I'll sit up and watch."

But Simon Belmont was already sleeping, snoring gently.

Tim looked upon the face of the hero in the torchlight, and saw how it had aged in this past day and a half. He was glad he didn't have a mirror. He didn't want to look at his own face. Although he'd always wanted to grow up, he didn't want to grow up that fast!

Still, he had matured. There was no question about that. He had learned lessons about life and about himself that he would never forget.

That was, if he ever got back home. How

he longed for the familiarity of his room, his comic collection, the grumbles of his parents, liver and onions once a week for supper. He even wished he was back in that bathroom at his junior high, waiting to confront Burt!

Burt was absolutely nothing compared to what he had faced in the last two days.

So he was just sitting there, shivering a bit, trying to warm his hands with the flame from the torch when the most trying time of the whole journey hit.

It came on slowly and subtly. Quite simply, Simon Belmont woke up.

"Simon! That was fast!" Tim hopped to his feet, wanting to get out of this dark and depressing place. "Let's go!"

Simon said nothing. He just looked at Tim with dark and brooding eyes.

"Simon? Are you okay, pal?"

Simon remained mute. He looked around, then smiled the most devilish, evil smile that Tim Bradley had ever seen.

"There is no Simon here, brat! This body is all mine now!"

Simon/Not Simon opened his mouth wider, revealing the sharpest, deadliest pair of fangs that Tim Bradley had ever seen.

"And now, if you would so kindly bare your neck, I am very, very thirsty!"

And with that, Dracula leapt upon Tim Bradley.

Now, Tim Bradley had seen many vampire films. He'd seen the likes of Bela Lugosi, Christopher Lee and many other actors portraying Dracula, and other evil creatures of the night whose profession was the oral removal of blood from the veins of human victims. He'd seen plenty of cinematic vampires leaping on people.

But actually experiencing it was quite different.

For one thing, as strong as Simon Belmont was in real life, possessed by the spirit of Dracula he seemed to have the strength of ten madmen. He grabbed Tim and threw him across the clearing, almost hitting a tree.

Tim staggered to his feet grabbing at his side for his whip. The initial attack had been so fierce, so violent, and above all, so quick that Tim had not even had the chance to pull out his whip and defend himself.

Now that he knew how to use it, he might as well!

He snapped it.

But with lightning speed, Dracula/Simon grabbed it and pulled it out of his hands.

"No help there, mortal!" The agate eyes gleamed a horrible enthusiastic fire.

Tim reached down to his belt to get whatever else he might have that might be of help. He came up holding something hard and round.

Ah! A bulb of garlic! That should do the trick!

"Get back I say!" he cried, brandishing the garlic.

"Yum!" said Dracula/Simon. He grabbed the garlic and popped it into his mouth, crunching it up through a big, fat grin. "My favorite!"

"*Yikes!*" said Tim. "I thought that vampires were supposed to hate garlic."

"I absolutely loathe the stuff. In fact, I daresay my body parts in the bag yonder are trembling with disgust. But you see, I'm in Simon Belmont's body, so it really doesn't affect me. I don't suppose you'd have another bulb, would you? I could just breathe on you and you'd die!" Dracula/Simon bent his head back and an absolutely hideous laugh escaped. "Ooooooooooh!" he exclaimed. "I am going to have such fun with you, little puny man!"

And he jumped again.

This time, Tim was ready for him. He leapt away, and the vampire charged past him, banging hard into a tree.

The vampire fell onto the ground. The experience did not faze him, however. He hopped right back to his feet and charged again, faster than before.

This time, his claws caught hold of Tim's coat. He pulled the teenager up to his face.

"Just a few pints," he said, drool splashing down onto his collar. "That's all I need."

"What's black and white and red all over?"

Dracula /Simon blinked.

"A newspaper!" yelled Tim.

Dracula/Simon did not make any expression.

But then, suddenly, the eyes were no longer flaring red. They turned a pale blue once more, and Simon Belmont — the true Simon Belmont — peered out.

"Simon!" cried Tim. "Simon! You're still in there! Fight him, man! Fight him!"

"I —" said Simon. "I'm fighting . . . fighting!"

But that was all that the hero could get out before his features bent once more and Dracula's fires smoldered in his eyes.

"A poor attempt!" said Dracula. "Besides, you fool, your stupid joke reserve is clearly running out. Even I in little Castlevania have heard that joke before."

The fangs came in closer, closer, and Tim could feel the hot breath of this monster who had taken over his friend.

This was it, he thought.

He's got me!

But then, just as Dracula's fangs were about to sink into the tender flesh of Tim Bradley, a most fortunate thing suddenly happened.

The first ray of dawn filtered through a break in the trees and touched Dracula/Simon's face.

The vampire screamed.

"Simon! Simon, fight him now," cried Tim. "Fight him!"

Tim could see the struggle going on in

his friend's face. Simon wrested himself from his clutch on Tim and hurled himself onto the ground.

"The Holy Water, Tim!" he said in a strangled cry. "Use the Holy Water!"

Yes, of course! The Holy Water! He should have thought of that before.

But then he realized why he had not.

He didn't know where it was!

"In my bag, Tim!" cried Simon. "Hurry! There's just enough left!"

Tim started for the bag, but then found himself tripping and tumbling to the ground. He looked around to see that Simon/Dracula had caught his pants leg and was trying to pull him back, even as the terrible struggle continued inside of Simon Belmont's body.

"No you don't!" said Tim. Angrily, he kicked him in the face! But Dracula hung on. Tim had to use all his might to drag himself and his burden to where Simon's bag sat.

He grabbed it, and rummaged around inside.

The flask! Where was the flask of Holy Water?

Dracula/Simon clawed his way up Tim's pants leg, ripping and tearing along the way.

Tim's hand grabbed something solid. Without waiting to unstopper the flask (or even checking to make sure it was a flask) Tim bashed his attacker across the noggin.

Liquid splashed out on him.

Simon/Dracula screeched. He writhed and squirmed.

But then he rolled into a shaft of light from the newborn sun. Tim could see the spirit of Dracula evaporate from Simon's body like black dew. Simon stood, dripping water and smiling.

"Thanks," he said. "I needed that!"

GAME HINT

Look for a secret compartment in the basement of the Mansion of Lauber.

CHAPTER NINETEEN

Storigoi Cemetery

"Do you think he's dead?"

Simon shook his head emphatically. "No."

"I don't know. When I threw that Holy Water on him, he looked like he was all shriveled. And look!" Tim gestured all around him. "I mean, it's already lighter ! I mean, before it was dark...all over. Even dark during the day! Surely that means that Dracula has been defeated."

"No." Simon held up the bag. "Until these parts are reassembled, until I confront Dracula again, in the flesh, and once more defeat him — and this time burn his body and thus send him back to the Dimension of monsters from which he is from — my beloved Castlevania will not be free of the dreaded curse of Dracula!"

"Well, you seem pretty sure about it, don't you," Tim shrugged. "I've come this far, I guess I can go the distance!"

"There's a good lad!" Simon Belmont was smiling. After all they'd been through, there was actually a grin on his face.

"You seem happy, Simon!"

"No, not happy, Timothy Bradley. I shall never be happy until Dracula has been banished from this land and Linda Entwhistle is again by my side!" Simon shook his head and clamped a brotherly hand on his assistant's shoulder. "It is you that I am happy with, my friend. You have renewed my faith not only in fortune, but in the human spirit!"

Tim could think of nothing smart to say to this. Actually, to tell the truth he was moved more than he could say. He looked up at Simon.

"I have a confession to make, Simon."

"Oh? Some little mistake of your youth?"

"I am not the strong-willed person that you think I am."

"I never said you were strong-willed, Timothy Bradley. Merely a good person."

"Well, my weaknesses almost betrayed us both."

He told about his experience with Dracula in the alley.

Simon listened carefully and patiently. And then he nodded. "I suspected as much?"

"You did? Why?"

"I didn't see you sneaking any of that chocolate candy of yours. I figured that you must have lost it somehow. I assumed that Dracula would tempt you."

"But why didn't you say something?"

"There are certain matters, Tim Bradley, that an individual can only take care of himself. However, be assured that if I had ever thought that you would not have been able to deal with the temptations of Dracula, I would have come to your support immediately and with all of my available powers." Simon put a reassuring hand on his friend's shoulder. "You must realize by now that none of us can make it through this life alone, Timothy Bradley. We all need each other's help!"

"Oh, yeah?" said Tim, grinning. "What about my video games? I do all those on my own."

"Ah, but did I not see a few *How To Score More Points* video tapes on your shelf?"

Tim blushed. "Well, uhm, er ... "

"As a great poet once said, 'No man is an island!' " said Simon with a wry expression.

"Well if that's the truth, Simon, then you must be a whole continent!"

Simon laughed good naturedly. "And you a whole world unto yourself, Timothy Bradley. And a very warped, twisted and fun world at that!"

"Thanks! I'll take that as a compliment!"

A little embarrassed, he looked around him, only realizing now exactly where they had come.

"It's a cemetery!" Tim exclaimed.

"But not just any cemetery!" Simon assured him. "It's Storigoi Cemetery!"

"Storigoi Cemetery!" said Tim. "But what does that mean?"

"Look about you, Timothy Bradley, and you shall surely see!"

So Tim looked.

At first glance it looked much like an old-fashioned cemetery. Tim shivered. It was all like a scene out of that movie *Beetlejuice,* only far more real and far scarier. He had not only run out of silly jokes and puns, he didn't feel like using them anyway.

This neither seemed the time nor the place.

"What are you talking about?" Tim asked, more than a little bit baffled.

"Look closer," said Simon. "Look at one of the graves."

Tim shrugged and peered closer at one of the closest graves.

HERE LIE THE MOLDERING REMAINS OF JACOB VARLEY, it said.

"So? I still don't see anything spec —"

Suddenly, hands sprouted from the sides of the gravestone and grabbed Tim Bradley by the shirt. A mouth formed in the gravestone. The hands pulled Tim closer.

"Yikes!"

Simon said. "Don't worry, Tim. It won't harm you."

The gravestone said, "Hey, kid. Boy, do I have a story to tell you! You wanna hear how I died? Or shall I start from the beginning?" The mouth flapped a large red tongue as it talked. "Okay. I was born in the Year of the Plum Pudding on Nardo Street. That's right to the left of the park, ya know? So then . . ."

Tim pulled himself away from the clutching hands.

"Hey, wait," said the grave. "I haven't finished my story! And boy is it a good one. Just give me a coupla' minutes of your time!

I swear you won't be sorry. It's an absolutely super tale!"

"Uh, maybe later." Tim looked at Simon. "I suppose you're about to tell me that every stone tells a story."

Simon nodded.

Gravely.

They both laughed.

"Hey!" called the next nearest gravestone, leaning forward insistently. "Don't listen to Jacob! All he did all his life was work in a shop! Me, I was an adventurer. I was also in the army. Boy, do I have some great stories to tell!"

"Actually," said Simon Belmont. "What we need now is some help. Some directions. We've got Dracula's body parts here but I've got to take them someplace special to assemble them and fight Dracula in person so that I can remove Castlevania's curse — to say nothing of my own."

"Ah," said another bigger gravestone with a bigger mouth. "These guys are really boring. Listen to my story and then we'll tell you what you're gonna have to do."

"I'm afraid we don't really have time," said Tim. "We've got until sundown tonight to do this and although its still kind of cloudy up there. It's well past noon!"

"*Pah!* Plenty of time!" said the Jacob grave. "And maybe I did have a boring life, but I'll tell you, the people who came into my shop brought some wonderful stories. Like the sailor who'd just taken a trip with none other than PegNose the Pirate! Now there's a story!"

"No, really!" insisted Simon. "We do need to get out of here and on our way!"

"No you don't"

"Listen to my story!"

"No! Listen to my story!"

"I've got tall tales to beat the band!"

The clamor in the cemetery was so noisy that Tim had to put his hands over his ears.

"Oh, dear," said Simon Belmont. "It looks as though I'm going to have to use the secret weapon here."

He held up the garlic necklace.

Immediately, there was silence.

"Ugh!"

"P.U.! Garlic!"

"Put it away!"

"Get that junk out of here!"

Simon waved the garlic, blowing the fumes out toward the assembled gravestones. "I will. But only if you will cooperate with us!"

"Okay!"

"Put those stinkballs away. We'll tell you what you want to know. Just get rid of that stuff."

Simon slipped the garlic back under his cloak. "Okay, then, gravestones. What do you have to say for yourselves?"

The gravestones of Storigoi Cemetery told them to take the top path through the woods.

Tim and Simon did so.

The gravestones told them that this top path would take them to the town of Andole.

Sure enough, the path did just that.

The talking gravestones told them to buy a morningstar in Andole. Tim had thought that they meant to actually purchase a planetary object. Simon explained patiently that a morningstar was a weapon — a heavy stick with a barbed ball at the end.

Sure enough, they found a member of the resistance movement against Dracula who supplied them with the needed weapon.

The final part of the mission was not as easy to understand.

"Tell me again," said Tim. "I'm not sure I heard those weird gravestones right."

"Oh, you heard them correctly," said Simon. "Next we have to catch a ride on a tornado!"

Tim sighed. "I was afraid that was what they said!"

And they headed away from the town of Andole toward their final appointment with Dracula.

GAME HINT

You must kill Thanatos.
Don't leave the room when you're in the middle of the fight or you'll just have to start over.

CHAPTER TWENTY

Deborah Cliff

All of the things they had collected lay in a pile on the ground by the edge of the cliff.

Except for the pieces of Dracula. Those were still in the sack, slung over Simon's shoulder. They would not part with it.

They were out in the open now, beneath a darkening sky. The clouds whirled around them as though the weather itself was aware of the importance of what was about to happen. Tim had absolutely no idea what would happen next. All he could do was just stick with Simon Belmont and trust in him.

They had been guided to the very edge of Castlevania — to that dark place known as Deborah Cliff where one dimension jutted into the next. There was the smell of sea here, and a massive mountain range rose along the horizon until it merged into the pure black of the stuff between universes. Lightning lashed at a distant nameless sea, and thunder crashed.

Simon Belmont prepared himself.

He carefully held the crystal that Linda Entwhistle had guided them to. It was red now. It sparkled and glowed.

"Here it is, Linda," said Simon. The power you invested in me. The faith and love you gave me. Here it is, I give it back. I give it back to Castlevania. I offer up everything to the powers of good in all the universe! Please! Send us now to the place where I can do my final battle with Dracula!"

Nothing happened.

Indeed, the crystal seemed to sparkle somewhat less. The waves stopped crashing, the wind stopped blowing, and the thunder and lightning stopped.

All was still.

Ominously still.

"What's happening?" asked Tim, unable to take the suspense anymore.

"*Shhhh!* Can't you hear it?"

"Hear what? I can't hear anything!"

"There it is!" Simon's eyes glittered with anticipation. "Off to the right, yonder."

Tim listened harder, and this time he did indeed hear something! It came down from the north like the howl of a lonely wolf. And even as he listened the sound grew louder, a sweeping yowling sound.

Then he saw it.

It was a white cone, whirling on its end, snarling and growling with a power that Tim had never even imagined before, much less witnessed.

A tornado!

And it was coming straight for them.

Tim's first instinct was to run.

Run and run just as fast as he could.

This was, in its way, far more terrifying than anything supernatural that he'd seen in the past two days. This was raw, elemental power. Power that could pick him up and smash him against a rock like a giant might crush a fly against a wall.

Simon grabbed him by the arm.

"No, Tim. It is frightening, I know. Terribly frightening." His long blond hair was whirling with the harsh whip of the wind, and he had to yell to make himself heard above the din. "But have faith. Trust."

Tim stopped himself. Yes. He had come this far. Now he had to do something that was, in its way, the most terrifying thing he'd done yet.

Which was to do nothing.

He had to trust. He had to stay still, and just surrender himself to something far greater than he was.

He had to trust the powers of good.

Ultimately, that was what he had fought for all this time, and that was what had fought through him against the darkness of Dracula.

And knowing that, Tim Bradley realized that there was both good and bad in himself, in everyone. But it was the ultimate responsibility of all people to allow good to work through them to the benefit of all.

It was an incredible revelation and its power and nobility swept through Tim Bradley, cleaning out all the old residue of doubt.

Still, he was scared, and Simon Belmont could clearly see that.

"Take my hand, Timothy Bradley!" the hero said. "Take my hand and together we shall face this final challenge. Victory is but a leap of faith away!"

Tim nodded. He reached out, but a gust of wind grabbed him and pulled him away.

"Tim!" cried Simon. "Take my hand! Take it, so that we will not be separated.

Tim struggled against the wind. It was gale force by now, close to a hundred miles an hour.

But somewhere, from deep down inside of him, there roared up the power that he needed.

He struggled.

He put all of his heart and soul into that struggle, and he reached out for Simon Belmont's hand.

And grabbed it.

A course of power seemed to flash through Simon's hand to his, and he took that power and used it to pull himself closer to his friend.

"Hold on, Tim! Hold on! Here it comes!"

Tim looked up and he could see the tornado bend over like a crazy Slinky toy. His first thought was to close his eyes, to just get away from this terrible thing. But he made himself stop.

No. He would face it. If this was his death coming down to him, then he would face it. He would face it with his friend.

The tornado dipped down and picked them up like toys, and flung them down into its throat.

Tim Bradley lost consciousness.

GAME HINT

As you walk through mansions, throw holy water on the floor to find pitfalls.

CHAPTER TWENTY-ONE

The Castle Tower

When he woke up, at first he did not know where he was.

He was laying on something hard. That much he knew. It was hard as stone, and it was cold.

In fact, as he turned over and reached out, he could see that in fact it was stone.

Tim groaned and looked up.

Above him the sky swirled harsh and mean, basically black with an over-tinge of red. The air was charged with electricity. There was the feeling of danger.

Cr-rack!

Simon's whip!

Tim looked around.

Sure enough, there he was, looking incredibly big, incredibly powerful, Simon Belmont, hero of Castlevania!

Simon cracked the whip again. Clearly, he was just practicing. Practicing for the final confrontation with Dracula.

"Tim," he said. "You're awake!"

"Yes ... but how ... where ..."

"I let you sleep. You needed the rest. We still have a half hour to go before sunset. I needed to prepare before I engage Dracula.

Loosen my muscles, prepare my spirit...."
He cracked the whip again.

Tim looked around to get his bearings. They were on the top of a castle tower. Tim could see the castle yard below. The farther spires were cloaked in a fine ghostly mist. Flags fluttered in a slight breeze.

"It's just like my dream!"

Simon looked up from his work with his whip. "Dream?"

"Yes, just before you came for me, that very morning I had a dream that I would be here on top of a tower very much like this." He walked to the parapet, touched the stone. "I guess you'd call that a premonition, wouldn't you?"

Simon grunted. He snapped his whip again. "And then again, perhaps your heart has always been here in Castlevania."

"I know my parents say that my brain is trapped in Nintendo land. But I don't know about my heart."

"This is a place of the heart, Timothy Bradley. It is a place of the spirit." He went to a bag in the middle of the circle that was the top of the tower. "But now, we must deal with more physical realities." He opened the bag and from it he drew out the five pieces of Dracula's body. These he placed in a pile. Then he drew out a wooden stake which he had purchased in Andole. Finally, he pulled out a jar of oil and some matches.

This time, Simon Belmont intended to do the job properly.

"Stand back, Tim Bradley. I am about to utter the spell given to me by Linda."

"The spell to bring Dracula's spirit back into his body."

Simon nodded grimly. "Are you prepared? Is your heart at peace with your maker. We may well die here on top of this tower!"

"We may well have died during the trip!"

"Yes, but the danger is greatest here. It is for good reason that only a tornado can bring you to the top of Castlevania's Death Castle. It is a dreaded and terrible place, a place where only the bravest may tread! For it is here that one faces that which he fears the most."

"And what is that for you, Simon?"

"I fear Dracula the most. Why do you think I stalk him so?" He shuddered and closed his eyes. "I have feared Dracula since I was a little boy. I was not born a hero, Timothy Bradley, but I have faced my fears. He who confronts his deepest dreads every day...that person is a hero." Simon stood further away. "So come, hero. Stand beside me as I chant these words. Join me as I make my final stand against Dracula!"

Tim walked up to Simon. "I am proud to do so, Simon. And I am proud to be your friend."

"Tell me, Timothy Bradley. What is your greatest fear now? What do you have to confront?"

Tim frowned. "I am afraid that I shall not be a good enough fighter."

"Fear not, Tim. It makes no difference. In this place it is not the skill with which one wields a weapon. It is the spirit and the will power behind the hero. And these, good friend, you do not lack." He turned and faced the pile of Dracula's parts and began to intone the chant.

> "By all that is good, and all that is bad
> Bring back Dracula to this place of the
>   sad.
> Conjure up his spirit from the air.
> And fill up his body . . . right there!"

Simon flung his whip end over the body parts. The effect was immediate and astonishing.

A bolt of lightning blasted down and struck the pile of Dracula's parts with a mighty explosion. White smoke billowed up around it like a shroud.

When it cleared, there stood the evil count himself—Dracula!

But he was not cowering, nor did he look at all afraid. For he had his arm around a beautiful woman, holding her as a man might hold a shield.

It was Linda Entwhistle!

CHAPTER TWENTY-TWO

The Final Confrontation:
Part Two

Although Tim had seen the face of Dracula before, he had never seen Dracula in his full physical glory.

And the sight was imposing indeed.

Somehow the parts of the count had come together and woven themselves into a creature that fairly glowed with good health. Count Dracula stood well over six feet tall. He looked like a body builder who used human blood as his after-workout cocktail.

His eyes blazed red and his cape shone with pure blackness. It was spread out behind him, like the wings of a bat.

Tim found himself incapable of coming up with any jokes or puns. In the presence of Dracula, it was difficult to imagine a world with anything funny in it at all.

"Linda!" cried Simon. "Linda, get away from him!"

"She can't!" said Dracula, eyes flaring.

"Dracula," said Simon. "I have fought against you all my life. I have to finish that fight now."

"Oh, dear, I was afraid you'd say that. Well then, I'm afraid that if you make even one little step toward me, then I'll have to end this young lady's life. And you wouldn't want that, would you?"

Simon lowered his whip.

"Simon! Don't!" called Tim. "All of Castlevania is at stake!"

Stake! That reminded Tim. The stake was still on the ground. If he could just pick it up ... If he could just sneak around ...

"I must surrender!" There were tears in Simon's eyes. "I cannot stand here and watch her die. I love you, Linda! I love you more than my own life!"

"That's right, Simon. Do think of priorities," snarled Dracula. "So then. Do we make a deal? Or are negotiations still in order?"

While Dracula was busy speechifying, Tim was busy sneakifying. Without attracting the vampire's attention, the teenager stepped over to the stake, picked it up, and began to creep up on Dracula from behind.

"There is nothing more to talk about!" said Simon. "You must leave Castlevania!".

"What? Banished from my kingdom!"

"No. Simply leave."

Dracula chuckled sourly. "Thanatos would boil me alive should I return to the dimension of monsters."

"Go somewhere else then."

"What? Earth? I didn't fare very well there. Not well at all. That is why I came to Castlevania. It's much more hospitable here. Why should I leave?"

"Because," said Tim. "You're such a jerk!"

And he ran with all his might toward Dracula.

The count turned and hissed. But the charge did catch him off guard, and he could not hang onto his captive. Linda Entwhistle, long dress and tresses fluttering, broke away and ran.

Tim pushed the stake toward Dracula's heart, but the vampire was too quick. He caught the wood in his powerful hand at the last moment, and he wrenched it away from the boy as easily as a diner might wield a toothpick. He tossed the stake over the side of the tower.

"Pah! Foolish mortal! You think that a stake will stop me?" He advanced toward Tim, claws outstretched.

Simon hurled his morningstar. It snapped on Dracula's arm and the count flinched, but he did not stop his advance. He grabbed Tim Bradley by the front of his shirt and he pulled him up so close that Tim could see the little grooves on the side of the vampire's fangs.

"I will deal with you later, Belmont. First, though, I wish to pay back a smaller debt!"

Tim felt helpless in such a powerful grip. But Dracula held him in such a way that Tim could reach into his own back pocket.

And he did just that, pulling out the little portable video game player that he'd snuck into school and promptly forgotten all about!

"What is that?" snarled Dracula, a look of alarm in his eye.

"Why, it's the latest thing from Earth, Dracula. Haven't you heard of it? A VAMPIRE ZAPPER!"

"A vampire zapper?" said Dracula. "Absurd."

"*Au contraire,* Drac. This, you see, is my secret weapon. Prepare to zapped!"

And Tim pressed the button.

The machine made a terrible series of sounds, and Dracula nearly jumped out of his skin. In just a moment, he would see that the device was harmless. But the distraction was just enough to give Simon the time he needed.

Thwack!

Dracula gasped. He looked down. Where there had once been only his suit and a clean white shirt, there was now a wooden stake sticking out.

"But," he gasped. "But ... I threw ... the stake ... away!" said Dracula as he weaved dizzily back and forth.

"I had an extra," said Simon.

The hero tossed the oil onto the count.

And he lit a match.

"Well," said Tim Bradley. "So much for Dracula! He certainly did pop off to his home dimension spectacularly, didn't he?"

"Yes," said Linda Entwhistle. She leaned into Simon Belmont's big chest, nuzzling. "And he didn't look very happy about it. But

I'm certainly glad to be at home. Especially now that I've got this!" She held up her hand. On her ring finger, in a setting of gold, was the very diamond that Simon had picked up along the way of the Quest. "It will be nice to have a husband. Especially a hero husband, but I suspect that husbands are much the same, hero or no hero!"

Simon looked a little puzzled but happy. Tim could only laugh.

They were sitting outside the inn now. It was a beautiful day. As soon as they had cast Dracula back to the dimension of monsters, all the clouds and the storm signs had blown away and the sun had come out, beautiful and golden.

With the help of a little magic, the heroes and the heroine had returned to their hometown, where there was great fanfare and celebration to meet them.

"I brought something for you, Tim," said Linda Entwhistle. "Something from the dimension where I was imprisoned that they don't have here, but that I know you like."

She pulled out a large bar of rich, brown milk chocolate.

Tim could feel himself about to drool at the very sight of this piece of deliciousness. Boy, he wanted to just take it in his mouth and chew it up and let the wonderful gooey stuff slide down his throat and —

Wait a minute.

No, he didn't.

Well maybe he did, but now he realized

that he had something far more wonderful than just a love for chocolate.

He had control.

He had a choice.

"Thanks, Linda. That's very nice of you, but I think I'll pass for now."

She smiled prettily at him. "Okay. I understand. I'm not really trying to tempt you, Tim."

"No. I realize that. It's just that it's nice to be able to say no."

"Well, Linda," said Simon. "I suppose it's about time for you to help Tim here get back home."

Home. The whole concept was different to Tim Bradley now. These past two and a half days in Castlevania had changed him so much, that he really didn't think of home in the same way anymore.

"Hey!" he said. "What's the hurry? Just let me stay here for a while longer. I mean, I'm just getting to know you guys. And I've not really gotten to know the real Castlevania, either . . . the sunny, happy Castlevania."

Linda shook her head sadly. "I'm afraid, Tim, that already your presence here is creating a wrong vibration in both Castlevania and on Earth. We'd like you to stay, Tim, but for everyone's sake it's best that you go."

Simon looked very troubled. "I shall miss you, Tim. You have been a good friend."

Tim nodded. He'd miss the big guy, too.

They shook hands.

"Oh, one little matter," said Tim. "As long as you seem to be able to shift dimensional time and space... I don't suppose you'd be willing to ship me back to someplace other than that boys' room where you found me. There's this huge guy named Burt outside the door waiting for me to come out."

Linda Entwhistle looked at Tim with less respect than Tim had hoped for. "Now, Tim. You have faced far scarier things than your junior high school rival here in Castlevania!"

"Yeah, but back there... that's reality."

"This has been reality, too, Tim," said Simon seriously.

"I know, but this is your reality. Back there... that's my reality."

"And don't you think that your reality back there has changed from your experiences here."

Tim thought about that.

"Yeah. I guess you're right. Still, I really don't want to face —"

"We must face all our problems, even the small ones," said Linda Entwhistle. "If we don't then we become our own problem."

"Okay, okay. But will I ever be able to come back."

"In many ways, Timothy Bradley," said Simon Belmont, "you will never leave."

They solemnly shook hands.

Linda Entwhistle took something out of her pocket. It was the crystal that had helped them so many times during their trip. Now it held a dazzling collection of rainbows inside. Linda whispered some words. A door appeared. Through it, Tim Bradley could see his own world.

Or rather, the tile walls of the boys' room of his junior high school.

"You will return just two seconds after you left," said Simon.

Tim took a deep breath and headed for the door.

"Tim," said Simon. "You really won't need the whip . . ."

"Rats!" said Tim. He took his weapons and handed them back to Simon. "I guess you're right, though. I'm going to have to face Burt with my bare fists."

Simon shook his head. "Tim, I realize that we have experienced much violence here in Castlevania. But that was a sad necessity. From what I can tell, back in your home world there is far too much violence. Perhaps you should try and deal with your rival in a different way."

"And you will be none the less a man for it!" promised Linda.

Tim sighed. "You're right."

He gave Simon another handshake and he gave Linda a hug and then he turned to the door between the dimensions.

"Oh, well," said Tim Bradley. "At least he's not Dracula."

"They are all Draculas," said Simon Belmont. "But they all can be bested, Tim. Remember that, and stay true to what you have learned in Castlevania."

Tim Bradley smiled, took a deep breath and stepped back into his own world.

Castlevania had been pretty rough, true.

But there really was nothing scarier — or more challenging — than junior high school!

Dear Reader,

I hope you liked reading *Castlevania II: Simon's Quest*. Here is a list of some other books that I thought you might like:

The Black Cauldron
by Lloyd Alexander

Bunnicula
by Deborah & James Howe

Dr. Jekyll and Mr. Hyde
by Robert Louis Stevenson

Eight Tales of Terror
by Edgar Allen Poe

The Eyes of the Dragon
by Stephen King

The Hobbit
by J.R.R. Tolkien

You can find these books at your local library or bookstore. Ask your teacher or librarian for other books you might enjoy.

Best wishes,

F.X. Nine

Enter the

WORLDS OF POWER™

GIVEAWAY!

WIN A NINTENDO™ GAME BOY™ COMPACT VIDEO GAME SYSTEM!

You'll *score big* if your entry is picked in this awesome drawing! Just look what you could win:

GRAND PRIZE:

A Nintendo® GAME BOY™ compact video game system

10 Grand Prize winners!

SECOND PRIZE:

A cool video game carrying case

25 Second Prize winners!

Rules: Entries must be postmarked by November 5, 1990. Winners will be picked at random and notified by mail. No purchase necessary. Void where prohibited. Taxes on prizes are the responsibility of the winners and their immediate families. Employees of Scholastic Inc; its agencies, affiliates, subsidiaries; and their immediate families not eligible. For a complete list of winners, send a self-addressed, stamped envelope to Worlds of Power Giveaway, Contest Winners List, at the address provided below.

Fill in the coupon below or write the information on a 3" x 5" piece of paper and mail to: **WORLDS OF POWER GIVEAWAY**, Scholastic Inc., P.O. Box 742, 730 Broadway, New York, NY 10003. Entries must be postmarked by November 5, 1990. (Canadian residents, mail entries to: Iris Ferguson, Scholastic Inc., 123 Newkirk Road, Richmond Hill, Ontario, Canada L4C365.)

Nintendo® is a registered trademark of Nintendo of America Inc. Game Boy™ is a trademark of Nintendo of America Inc. **WORLDS OF POWER** ™ Books are not authorized, sponsored or endorsed by Nintendo of America.

Worlds of Power Giveaway

Name _____ Chris morton _____ Age ___ 9 ___

Street _____ North Woods Cir. _____

City _____ Chardon _____ State Oh Zip 44029

Where did you buy this _Worlds of Power_ book?

☐ Bookstore ☐ Video Store ☐ Discount Store ☐ Book Club

☑ Book Fair ☐ Other_____ (specify) WOP190